The temptation to use Nicole to get back at her father was strong.

It drove Jake to relentlessly pursue her, helped by the attraction sizzling between them.

Jake no longer wanted to kill Nicole's father, as he had in his youth. Now he had a more subtle weapon of revenge. He was going to watch Mike Bradley squirm with the knowledge that Jake Slater wanted his daughter. Jake was sure Nicole knew nothing of what had happened all those years ago. He would just capitalize on her ignorance and let it work for him. He just wondered how far he was willing to go.

There was only one catch. Nicole wasn't what Jake had expected. Her vulnerability spawned a rough tenderness in him that he didn't know what to do with. *Don't let emotions creep into this,* he warned himself. Nicole's father had this coming....

Dear Reader,

As always, I'm very proud of the lineup of books we're offering this month in Silhouette Intimate Moments. I think every story here is exciting, and every author is writing at the top of her form. But there's one book I'd especially like to discuss in more detail, taking a somewhat more serious tack than I usually do.

For many years I have been closely involved with Silhouette Intimate Moments, having a strong voice in choosing what books we'll bring to you, then scheduling those books, and also handling the reader mail I'm so lucky to receive from so many of you. Over the years, one question has been asked of me many times. Sometimes the letter writer identifies herself as black, sometimes as a woman of color, sometimes as an African-American. But always the question is the same: Why aren't you publishing books about women like me, black women meeting and falling in love with black men? Always my correspondent tells me that she enjoys our books anyway—a compliment I am happy to receive on behalf of all our talented authors—but that just one book about a black couple would make her happy, make her feel that she belongs fully to the fellowship of readers spanning the globe. This month I am proud to be bringing you—all of you, whatever the color of your skin—*Unforgivable* by Joyce McGill. *Unforgivable* is a sizzling novel of suspense, of small-town secrets and sensuous romance. It is a novel for every woman, every reader of Silhouette Intimate Moments, because the emotions in it are universal, just as love is. And I hope that all of you—whatever your heritage, whatever the color of the face that looks back at you from the mirror—will read this terrific book. It is a book I'm proud of, just as I'm proud of every book we publish. But in this case I feel a special sense of pride, because it gives all of us a chance to prove what the sages have told us down through the years: Love is indeed blind. It recognizes no boundaries of color, of country, of language or of age. Love is always love, and all of us can share its bounty.

Thank you all for listening, and for the support you have so freely given over the years. And I promise to be back next month with more exciting—and I suspect unexpected!—news.

Leslie Wainger
Senior Editor and Editorial Coordinator

JOANNA MARKS

Wild at Heart

SILHOUETTE·INTIMATE·MOMENTS®

Published by Silhouette Books New York

America's Publisher of Contemporary Romance

SILHOUETTE BOOKS
300 East 42nd St., New York, N.Y. 10017

WILD AT HEART

ISBN: 0-373-07443-3

First Silhouette Books printing August 1992

Printed in the U.S.A.

Books by Joanna Marks

Silhouette Intimate Moments

Love is a Long Shot #315
Wild at Heart #443

JOANNA MARKS

didn't realize it at the time, but she prepared early to be a novelist. In the second grade, according to her teacher, she entertained her class with her stories. She's still concocting stories, now romances. She has spent time in England, Libya and Colombia, and currently lives in Florida.

Chapter 1

"What will it be, Nicole?" the bartender inquired.

"A soda with a twist of lime."

He nodded and wiped the gleaming mahogany bar and moved away. Nicole felt pleasantly tired after a busy Friday in the newsroom. She had just completed a series on the Miami Police Department that had been appearing in the newspaper all week. She felt the afterglow of a job well-done and decided to rest on her laurels and bask in its warmth. While she waited for her drink, Nicole glanced idly around the crowded lounge. Oscar's Bar and Lounge was a favorite watering hole for journalists. This time of the day it was always packed with reporters, feature writers and editors winding down the workday before going home. The bartender returned with the drink and placed it on a neat white blotter.

"I'll have a bourbon on the rocks," the man at her side announced to the bartender. Malcolm Rogers, city editor for the *Miami Guardian,* calmly lit a cigarette.

The doors to the club swung open, and a man walked in. Nicole watched him out of idle curiosity at first. Good-looking in a lethal kind of way, tall, broad shouldered and powerfully built, he soon held her gaze like a magnet. She knew lots of good-looking men, but there was something about the man shouldering his way through the crowd that made him stand out. What was it about him? she wondered. Intrigued, she studied him over the rim of the glass. Aroused feminine speculation ran through her in deep dark streams.

He looked lean, mean and macho and *very* predatory. He was definitely after someone or something, she concluded. Wondering who or what it was, she put her drink back down on the bar with an absent-minded air. Malcolm nudged her with his elbow. As she leaned toward him his droll voice rolled into her ears in conspiratorial tones, and Nicole realized that she wasn't the only one observing the unidentified man.

"See the man talking to the manager, the one who just walked in the door?"

"I see him. He doesn't look exactly burdened down with charm," she said, laughing softly. "Who is he?"

"That's Jake Slater. In that series you just finished, I seem to remember you labeling him something colorful. Now what was it ... ?"

"South Florida's deadliest cop." The face and name suddenly came together in her mind. Of course. Why had she not recognized him? Probably because she had never seen him before in the flesh. When she was researching the series and tried to interview him, he had always been too busy to see her, out covering or leading some investigation. In the series she had cited him as a first-rate homicide detective, one of the new breed—better educated, more dedicated, with a better developed sense of values. But he had also shot eight men, killed four and fought so many gun duels he probably couldn't remember them all. It was because of his impressive record that she had singled him out as South Florida's deadliest cop. She and Malcolm both kept their eyes on him as Slater talked to the manager. They were both drawing the same conclusion.

"That's trouble coming this way," Malcolm announced dryly.

"How do you know him?"

"I worked the police beat for more than a year. I got to know him pretty well. I know when he's not happy about something, and he doesn't look too happy right now."

Some people stepped aside to clear a space for him. With an upward sideways glance the first thing Nicole noticed was Jake Slater's eyes, which were steel gray, glittering with irritation and focused on Malcolm. While Slater's attention was diverted Nicole studied him. He didn't acknowledge her presence, though she sensed he was very much aware of it, as he was of everything else that went on around him. Assertive power flowed in waves from his eyes and his rugged, leanly muscled physique. Every feminine instinct she possessed told her he was a man of strong sexual magnetism. He propped his hands on his hips, conveying an air of barely controlled patience. His silvered brown hair reminded her of a desert fox. Closely cropped, it enhanced the lean sharp edges of his face, reinforcing its character and its macho masculinity.

"Hello, Malcolm."

"Hello, Jake. How's it going?"

In response, the first edition of the *Miami Guardian* slammed down hard on the bar, and Nicole raised an assessing eyebrow as she winced inwardly. It was going to be a bumpy evening.

"Who the hell is N. Bradley, Malcolm? Are you responsible for this series?" An impatient tanned finger tapped the inside page.

Out of the corner of her eye she watched Malcolm lift his hands in a gesture of innocent protestation. "I had nothing to do with the series. I've been away on vacation in Europe, Jake. I only just got back yesterday. You know, Italy is really nice this time of year. Not so many tourists—"

"Save it, Malcolm," Slater's low-pitched voice snapped.

Malcolm's eyes slid furtively toward Nicole while a phantom smile tugged at the corners of his mouth. "This is the person you want to speak to."

Nicole watched Jake Slater's irritated gaze slide slowly her way. Pinpoints of steel focused on her face. Something between her and Slater ignited. An electric sting danced along her veins. It was like a match head flaring deep inside her.

"The *N* stands for Nicole," she announced, focusing catlike green eyes on him. With her own brand of laid-back charm she smiled pleasantly at him. A smile was supposed to ease the way and oil the wheels of social intercourse, so she dragged up what she thought was one of her best ones, hoping to see an answering gleam. Motionless, he stared back at her with such chilling assessing male silence that for a moment she thought she was in danger of getting a case of frostbite.

"So you're the one who wrote this."

"That's right. Does something about it bother you?"

"Yeah. Something about it *bothers* me." He spoke in a lazy-toned drawl, emphasizing each word as if she were mentally subnormal and might have difficulty grasping his meaning.

"Like most people in this world I've got a job to do. I'm a detective. That means I carry a gun. When necessary I use it. I risk my life every day of the week. It's all part of the job and I accept that. What I don't accept is when some *hotshot female reporter* indulges in florid prose at my expense."

It wasn't so much what he said as the way he said it. He ground out the words *female reporter* as if she had hit rock bottom in his estimation, as if she were only a breath away from walking the streets.

Her green eyes flashed a silent warning at him. "My so-called florid prose is backed up with hard facts. You've been involved in more shoot-outs than any other cop on record. You have killed four men."

"I know how many men I've killed. I don't need you to remind me."

"Police records show that you are in fact the deadliest cop on the force. And while I have your undivided attention I would like to add that I'm about as

keen on macho cops as you are on hotshot female reporters.''

Gray eyes hardened lazily. A muscle flexed in the
lean cheek and adamant jaw.

''I want a retraction of some kind or a formal apology printed in tomorrow's edition. I'm holding you
responsible since it was you who dreamed up this gar-
bage.'' He jabbed an aggressive finger toward her
nose. She pulled back slightly, glaring at him.

God. Sometimes she couldn't stand cops. No one
would ever guess she was a cop's daughter. Though
she had spent most of her life around cops, her feelings about them were ambivalent. On the one hand she
loved them and respected them. On the other, she had
always sworn never to get involved with one. But she
understood how their minds worked. They were always highly wary around reporters, and she knew this
one especially felt threatened, so she attempted to
mollify him.

''The *Miami Guardian* has nothing to apologize for.
Police records show you're the best from all ac-
counts. Something of a living legend. I was only citing your efficiency when I pinned that label on you. I
meant nothing more than that you are a first-rate
homicide detective. You wouldn't want me to lie,
would you, or to distort the truth?'' She widened her
eyes with a look of mock innocence.

''Listen, Sunshine. When some half-asleep mem-
ber of the public reads this over their morning coffee,
what do you think is going to stick in their minds? A
hardworking homicide detective trying to do a difficult, often very tedious job?'' He shook his head
slowly. ''The image that's going to stick is of a trig-

ger-happy cop who shoots at anything that moves. I don't feel like having to defend myself over and over again to the Civil Liberties Union. They've been on my back more than once trying to pull my badge." He paused. Nicole stared back at him with bland insolence.

"I want that retraction, honey. And one way or another I'm going to get it." The hard-edged gleam in his eyes suggested the lengths he might go to get it.

She forced a fixed smile on her face to hide the effect those eyes had on her and to hide the fast-burning fuse of her temper. Without thinking, she jabbed a finger at his chest. "Don't patronize me, Detective Slater. I've told you my name. It's Nicole Bradley, not Sunshine or Honey."

Her jabbing finger activated Slater's legendary reflexes. With a bone-crushing grip his hand seized her wrist. A tiny animal cry of surprise burst from her lips while his lethal gray-eyed stare ate into her skin like a powerful acid.

Malcolm, who had stayed on the sidelines calmly sipping his drink, wisely intervened. "Calm down, Jake."

"Who says I'm not calm." The words were forced through tight lips while Nicole, stunned, watched in a daze. But Jake never took his eyes from her face. The strength of his hand burned into her flesh.

"I'm sure Nicole meant no offense. It might interest you to know, Jake, that Nicole's father is a cop in the Miami Police Department. She wouldn't intentionally go out of her way to offend one."

"Wouldn't she?" A disbelieving look accompanied the question.

"I'll personally see that the retraction is printed in the Monday edition," Malcolm said.

"See that *Sunshine* here writes it," Slater said ominously, fanning Nicole's temper.

She had never met a man more arrogant, she thought, staring silently back at him. But there was something about this hard-bitten detective with the eyes that echoed aeons of experience that dragged up reluctant admiration. He was a real hard case, someone who had seen a lot, but someone who somehow had managed to keep intact those qualities most admired in a man. Apparently satisfied that he had subdued her temporarily, he released the bone-crushing grip on her wrist. She rubbed the sore area, trying to get the circulation going again while she sensed Malcolm needling her with his eyes.

"All right. You'll have your retraction. Would you like it in *blood?*" she taunted softly, slanting him a look.

Peering down at her, his eyes danced with grim male humor. "Just to prove to you what a nice guy I can be, you can do it in cold type, honey."

Her soft mouth bent into a reluctant curve of amusement that was the closest she could come to a smile of acquiescence. Lifting her eyes slowly, she realized that he was studying her again with the same chilling male assessment she had seen before. But this time there was something else burning in his eyes.

"You're not related to Mike Bradley by any chance, are you?"

Something about his tone made her feel uncomfortable. Her expression became guarded. "I'm his daughter," she supplied. His irises crystallized for a fleeting moment as he digested that piece of information. Then his expression was enigmatic. She sat perfectly still trying to evaluate the puzzling look in his eyes. Slowly, something inside him eased off. He was looking at her differently now, as if seeing her in a completely different light. The atmosphere between them underwent a subtle but very profound change, yet it was hard to pinpoint how. She had no more time to consider the change in his expression because Malcolm intervened again.

"Look, Jake. Nicole meant no offense. As Mike Bradley's daughter, she obviously appreciates the difficulties that face the homicide detective, or any policeman for that matter. I saw the last of the series in this morning's paper. She did an excellent job on this series, by the way. I don't think it was offensive. It simply states that you're an outstanding homicide detective, and she used the somewhat unfortunate epithet in that context."

Jake ignored Malcolm. "So, you're Mike Bradley's daughter," he repeated as if he were having some trouble coming to terms with that fact.

"Yes. Is there something odd about that?"

"No. It surprises me, that's all. A cop's daughter being a reporter," he remarked dryly. "Somehow the two don't go together."

Nicole stared at him for a lingering moment, silently evaluating his words. Somehow she suspected there was more to his reaction than that.

"Why don't you join us for a drink, Jake?" Malcolm hailed the bartender. Nicole realized Malcolm, too, had seen something in Slater's attitude ease and change.

"Thanks," he responded. Though he had brushed aside the fact that she was Mike Bradley's daughter as being unusual only because of her professional status, she could still see the wheels turning in his head. They reminded her of steel wheels, matching the glint in his eyes. He hooked a bar stool with one of his long legs and dropped into it.

The bartender loped down to their end of the bar, and as he wiped the surface in front of them with a towel, he asked Jake what he wanted. Both Malcolm and Jake ordered drinks, while she sat quietly. She felt Jake's curious gaze linger, drinking in everything about her as if he were saving it all somehow for future reference. The bartender poured their drinks.

"I'm thinking of assigning Nicole to the police beat," Malcolm said. "With her background I think she'd be a natural for it. Don't you?"

Jake shot Malcolm a lazy look of contempt. "You worked that beat, Malcolm, for more than a year. It's no place for a woman. The hours are crazy. She can forget about having weekends off. The scene of a crime can be dangerous."

When his gaze returned to lock with hers, Nicole would have had to be blind to miss the awakening male interest. But even if she were blind she would still have felt it coming at her in waves. His initial attitude had vanished. In its place was undisguised male interest in an attractive female. A complete turnaround had been executed.

"She should be working the desks," Jake continued, reaching for his drink. "Climbing the editorial ladder, not out on the streets racing from one homicide to the next."

So he wanted her tucked safely behind a desk, did he. Nicole's slender eyebrow lifted at the suggestion. Recently Malcolm had been trying to lure her into covering the police beat because he felt she had a natural instinct for it. Up till now she had refused, knowing the crazy irregular hours of the beat and the basic mistrust of the press that was prevalent throughout the force. She had no desire to experience either one. But now, with Macho Man sitting in front of her, she felt like being assigned to it out of sheer orneriness. His words prompted her to make a few comments of her own on the subject.

"Women have covered the police beat before. It's not unheard of. In fact they can be very good at it. Women are usually more sensitive and intuitive, they pay more attention to detail and they have more empathy for the relatives of the victim."

He looked at her assessingly.

"I don't like to see a woman exposed to the grittiness of homicides, even if she is a cop's daughter. A woman should be shielded from that side of life. That is, unless you want a woman to become as tough as an old boot."

The look in his eyes made Nicole suddenly feel breathtakingly feminine and in need of constant male protection from the harshness of life. Was this the same man who only moments ago had crushed her arm with his steely grip, the same one who looked as though he would have taken great delight in strangling her with his bare hands? The thoughts running through her mind must have shone forth in her eyes. A look of teasing sensuality stole across Jake Slater's lean, handsome face.

"Maybe I'm wasting my breath, Malcolm. It could be I'm talking to one of those women who really wants to be a man."

Malcolm choked on his drink. Jake Slater was teasing her openly now, trying to get another rise out of her. There was a challenge in his eyes that was difficult to ignore, and Nicole found it impossible not to rise to the bait.

"Do I look like a man, Detective Slater?" She packed a lot of ammunition behind those words. Long legged, with a figure that went in and out in all the right places, she challenged his remark quietly. This was proving to be great fun because she liked nothing better than taunting one of these macho types by turning on a little sensual heat. She wasn't letting him get away with a remark like that. But Nicole had underestimated the man opposite her if she thought he would let her get away with anything.

"I never said you looked like one, honey, only that maybe you wanted to *be* one."

Her face burned under the impaling thrust of his eyes as he made her feel as if her femininity was at stake and that maybe she'd like to step outside and prove it. She had just made an important discovery. When Jake Slater hit back, he hit back hard.

"For the record, I do *not* want to be a man," she said evenly, her composure recovered.

The shadow of a smile crept around his mouth and into his eyes. "I'm relieved to hear that." He unwound his frame from the bar stool and stood over her intimidatingly. "Now that we got that out of the way, why don't we have dinner together on Saturday night?"

His words stunned her. He had been two steps ahead of her all the time. It was the retort she least expected, but she should have seen it coming. She had been neatly set up. For one long dizzying moment in the lengthening silence between them she found she wanted to say yes. What was wrong with her? Go out with this arrogant macho gorilla on a date? She must be losing her mind. That unpalatable knowledge suffused her face with an embarrassing warmth she couldn't hide. His eyes shone with the silent knowledge that for a fleeting moment at least part of her had wanted to say yes. That knowledge didn't seem to surprise him the way it did her.

Scrambling to recover she pushed out a confused reply. "I'm sorry, I won't . . . I mean can't."

"Can't or won't?" he prompted with amused satisfaction. "There's a difference."

"I can't."

He shot her a measuring look that said at some time in the future he would like to change that reply but he didn't have the time or the inclination right now. Instead he smiled enigmatically.

To her surprise she found herself fascinated and inexplicably attracted to this tall, outrageous man while at the same time silently loathing him. But she knew one thing for certain. He intrigued her more than any man she had ever met before. But there was another reason why she said she wouldn't go out to dinner. That reason had a name—Richard. Somehow she didn't think Richard would be very understanding if she went out on a dinner date with the imposing detective standing in front of her. She and Richard had a kind of unspoken agreement. The answer had to be no. She was still wrestling with her conscience and trying to come to terms with her initial reaction when Jake Slater's eyes locked hers with his as he made ready to leave.

"I'll be looking for the retraction in Monday's paper. If I don't see it, there will be hell to pay." Jake shoved his barely touched drink onto the bar.

"It will be in all the editions on one of the inside pages," Malcolm said reassuringly. "You have my word on it."

"It was *nice* meeting you, Nicole."

"*Nice* meeting you." She kept her expression blank but there was a bemused look in her eyes. The word *nice* sounded a bit anemic when she searched her mind to describe a first encounter with South Florida's deadliest cop, but for the time being it would have to do.

"See you around, Jake," Malcolm called out affably.

She watched Jake walk out the door, fascinated by the animal grace of his movements.

Malcolm turned around and grinned mercilessly. "I can see you really hit it off with Miami's most brilliant homicide detective."

Nicole shot him a wry look. "Strong personalities always generate sparks," she retorted with a blasé air, even though inside she felt unaccountably shaky.

"Watch out for Jake. I think he's interested in you. He'll hunt you down and he'll pull you in," Malcolm announced dryly. "He's had a string of women. I've heard he goes after them the same way he goes after some of his prime suspects." Malcolm laughed deep in his throat at his own joke. Somehow Nicole didn't find his remarks very funny so she remained silent.

Leaning back expansively against the bar Malcolm assumed a reminiscing posture. "You know, when I covered the police beat I got to know him as well as anyone gets to know him. Jake's a pretty amazing guy. Some people say he's got some kind of sixth sense for sensing trouble. It's either that or countless coincidences that explain all the thugs and killers he's pulled in. Everyone who knows him says he's the guy they want on their side when trouble comes around. He's also got a reputation for telling people exactly what's on his mind."

She wished Malcolm would either be quiet or change the subject, but he only ruminated some more.

"Jake makes the city fathers sweat. They live in fear of lawsuits and bad press. They never know what he's going to do next. He's been called on the carpet more times than I can count, but he's always been cleared of all charges. I guess that's why he's been so touchy about this label you stuck on him." Malcolm tapped the newspaper still lying on the bar.

"When I covered the police beat," he went on, "the men who worked with him told me that he's got split-second reflexes and a deadly aim. There's no time to stop and think when you fire a gun. It's all instinctive. Your description was apt even if he doesn't like it much, but we'll have to print an apology. I can see his point, though it never occurred to me when I read the copy this morning that he would take offense."

When Nicole got home she tossed her bag onto the small table next to the sofa and started unbuttoning her suit jacket. With it hanging open she walked through to her bedroom, unfastening her skirt. Heedlessly abandoning both pieces of clothing, she dropped them onto the floor, then shed her underclothes in the same manner, and walked slowly toward the shower. It was all done with an absentminded air.

In moments the warm spray pelted her face and careered down her soft curves as she twisted and turned luxuriating in its warmth. For a few blissful minutes her mind was blank. Languidly she began to soap her face and arms. With her eyes closed thoughts of the day began flickering into her mind. The water cascaded all around her, shrouding her, drowning out all the sounds and distractions of the world and leaving her mind vulnerable. The image of Jake Slater slipped its way in uninvited.

She searched in vain for some neat pigeonhole to put him into, but her mind couldn't come up with one. He was one of a kind. He was intriguing. There was something about him that had definitely gotten to her, but she wasn't sure what it was. Whatever it was, he had scored some direct hits at her sensual responses and something deep inside her. Malcolm was right. He had deadly aim in more ways than one. With amazing skill he had an unerring eye for knowing where and how to breach her defenses. What would happen now? Probably nothing. He was one of those people who walked into and out of your life. Even though he had made a strong impression, she never really expected to see him again, especially after she turned down his invitation. Though, come to think of it, he hadn't seemed bothered by her rejection.

As she was tying the sash of her terry-cloth robe around her waist, the front door to the condo slammed shut and she knew it was her father coming in. She pulled off the towel wrapped around her head, letting her hair cascade around her face, and walked out to meet him.

"Hi, Dad," she announced breezily. Standing on tiptoes she kissed him on the cheek, resting a hand on each shoulder.

Mike Bradley grunted a hello in reply. Still good-looking though he had just turned fifty, he gazed affectionately down at his daughter for a moment before he turned and picked up the newspaper. Then he moved toward his favorite chair, which no one else was allowed to sit in. He looked preoccupied. There was a weariness around his eyes that said he'd had a rough day.

"Hungry?"

"I could eat a horse."

"I'm just going to start dinner," she announced and watched him unsnap his shoulder holster strap and drop it onto the coffee table near the sofa. Her father had been with the police department for almost twenty years. He would be retiring soon. Somehow she couldn't imagine her father retired. He was too vital, too full of life, and he loved his job. She walked into the kitchen with that thought in her mind.

"Richard's coming over," she called out from the kitchen as she heard her father switch on the television. "Do you want to wait for him? We can all have dinner together."

"When's he coming?" Mike's voice boomed from the living room. "I had a terrible day. There was no time to stop and eat a decent lunch."

"Within the hour."

"I guess I can wait until then," he growled. She knew he didn't like the idea of waiting for dinner, but he did like Richard, and he was pushing hard for Richard to become his son-in-law. So far he hadn't had any luck.

"When are you going to marry that guy, Nicole, and put him out of his misery? You might as well. He spends more time over here than he does at his own place."

In the kitchen, where he couldn't see her expression, she smiled to herself at her father's gruffness. He never pulled any punches or dressed things up. He always said exactly what was on his mind.

"Is there anything going on between you two besides having dinner together?" he went on.

Her face turned warm. The innuendo in his tone was unmistakable. She put cut-up potatoes and other vegetables into a pot and turned on the heat. She moved to the doorway of the living room, leaning indolently against the doorjamb, and looked down at her father. He was sprawled in the chair with his feet up on a leather ottoman. She decided to tell him what she thought of his impertinent question.

"What kind of a question is that? That's not the kind of question a father asks his daughter." Her father had the good grace to look a little bit uncomfortable. But it wasn't in his nature to back down on anything. Part of her saw the funny side of it. Sensing her presence, her father angled his steel-gray head sideways to look up at her, with one hand on the remote control. His blue eyes were alive with the knowledge that he was embarrassing her.

"Okay," he conceded. "It's the kind of question a mother asks her daughter." He punched the remote to flip over to another channel, as if to punctuate what he was saying. "Your mother's been dead for a long time, Nicole, so I'm doing the asking." He looked at her candidly. "My instincts tell me no."

She gazed down at him with tolerant amusement. Her father had always been shrewd when it came to sizing up people. He had a natural talent for it, and his job had honed that natural talent to a fine edge. Ruefully she remembered she was never able to put anything over on her father. He was too quick.

"Your instincts are sound. Richard is a gentleman. He respects me. He wants to do the right thing and wait until we're married . . . *if* we marry."

Her father laughed softly. "Are you going to marry Richard or just feed him dinners for the rest of his life? I'm beginning to think Richard might be something else besides a gentleman," he muttered, then punched the button on the remote again.

Nicole looked at her father, her eyes widening at the insinuating remark. "Sometimes you really amaze me. You're not like the fathers one reads about in books."

"No, I'm not," he replied wearily. "I'm human, with all the shortcomings of any human being. So don't put me up on any pedestal, or expect me to live up to some image in a book. But I know something about human nature. Couples in love don't hang around together dragging their heels. Unless they can't afford to get married. If that's not the problem, then what *is* the problem?''

"I'm not sure about Richard or about me," she said quietly. What she really meant was she wasn't sure about her own feelings regarding Richard. She looked down at her father. His eyes searched her face.

The tone of his voice didn't alter and remained glib. "You've been going out with Richard for more than a year, Nicole. How sure do you have to be?''

"Very sure," she retorted, turning away again. "Besides, I like my job, and I'm not even sure I want to get married to *anyone*. When you pressure me it makes me less inclined to think about it at all.''

"In my book, women should be married and have children. It's just the way things should be.''

It was a waste of breath to argue with her father when he made up his mind. He muttered something under his breath she couldn't catch. She heard the television volume turn up with the evening news, and she disappeared into the kitchen to find the vegetables boiling over. She turned down the heat and put some steaks on to grill. While she waited for the steaks to broil and the vegetables to finish cooking, she leaned her head against the cabinet door, thinking about her father's question.

It wasn't the first time he had asked her about Richard, and it wouldn't be the last. She loved her father, but he could be pushy and bossy. He liked to throw his weight around when it meant getting something he wanted. He *wanted* to see her married, and he wanted grandchildren someday; he had informed her of that on more than one occasion. Well, there was nothing wrong with his wanting those things, but she wasn't ready. She continued standing there, day-dreaming about her career and about how she wasn't really ready to settle down, when the buzzer on the timer went off, jolting her out of her thoughts.

Simultaneously, a tall, lean man with serious brown eyes walked silently into the kitchen. Nicole was still on edge thinking about what her father had said, and the unexpected intrusion added to her edginess.

"How's my favorite reporter?"

"Hi," she said, trying to cover up her irritation.

"What are you doing?"

"Daydreaming and waiting for dinner to cook."

"About me, I hope," Richard said with a small smile. He wore glasses with thin tortoiseshell frames. He also wore an impeccably cut suit tailored by some exclusive men's store in Palm Beach. Richard was a stickler about appearance and always looked immaculate even on the hottest days. She had never seen him look untidy, let alone sloppy. The same could be said about everything else in his life. There were no loose ends; everything was always neat and concise, well thought out, well planned. His tastes were conservative, refined and cultured. To top it all off he was well on his way to a brilliant career in a prestigious law firm, expecting to be made a partner in the not too distant future.

Not for the first time did she wonder what he saw in her. She knew that her looks were not a disadvantage and that he was attracted more to career-minded women than homebodies. But she was also well aware of their glaring differences. Nicole had a wild streak buried deep inside her that she did her best to conceal from him, while Richard was all cool and regulated, inside and out. Nicole went peacefully along in life for long periods at a time, and then, without warning, occasional emotional eruptions flashed to the surface, wreaking havoc. Richard seemed to have no trouble at all keeping his emotions on an even-tempered keel. Maybe it was the old case of opposites attracted to each other, but then why was she dragging her heels? Coming up behind her, he put his hands on her waist, prompting her to answer his question.

"In a way, I *was* daydreaming about you."

"In a way? What's that supposed to mean?" he asked quietly, but his voice held the analytical tone of a lawyer turning over a question in his mind.

"I was thinking about how long we've been going together." Her voice dropped a notch, because her father's words had gotten to her, whether she liked to admit it or not.

"That situation can easily be remedied. I've suggested numerous times that we become engaged and then get married. We can end this 'going together' any time you say. Why the serious expression tonight?"

The incident at Oscar's Bar came into her mind as he nuzzled the side of her neck. "Oh, I'm just a little tired. I had a long, hectic day and at the end of it I had a confrontation with an irate homicide detective."

"Did you shoot him down in flames?" Richard laughed softly. "A cop's daughter should be able to make mincemeat out of a detective. You know all their weaknesses and all their fears." A trial lawyer, Richard always saw things in courtroom perspective.

"Well, I *was* holding my own for a while," she said, remembering. "Then I had to give in to that jumped-up gorilla since I wanted to keep my job. At first he was really uptight about something I had written—I dubbed him South Florida's deadliest cop. Then Malcolm promised to print an apology in Monday's paper. But the funny thing was when Malcolm told him I was a cop's daughter—*Mike Bradley's* daughter seemed to be what made the difference—his whole attitude toward me changed somehow. It was really odd," she finished with a bemused, distant look in her eyes.

Richard's hazel eyes were considering when he turned her around in his arms. "Are you sure you're not reading too much into it? The explanation seems fairly simple and straightforward to me. I suspect he probably realized that you didn't mean it as some kind of slur, but as a compliment to his efficacy at his job. That is how you meant it, isn't it?"

"Yes, that's right. I just meant that he was something of a legend on the force. The other men respect him. He's considered to be the best."

"And he didn't take it that way at first?"

"No, absolutely not."

"But when he discovered that you were the daughter of a law enforcement officer, that put a different complexion on things. Now that you're printing an apology, everything's going to be all right."

"I guess you're right," she agreed with an absent-minded air, but still felt vaguely dissatisfied with the explanation.

"What's for dinner?" he queried softly.

"Steak." She smiled, knowing it was his favorite.

"Sounds good to me." He grinned.

"So how's my favorite up-and-coming attorney?"

"Hungry. And I've got a brief to work on tonight, but I made time to see you, which only goes to show how you've got me twisted around your little finger."

Nicole grabbed hold of his tie and tugged on it playfully so that he was forced to lower his head. "You're a nice guy, you know that?" She breathed the words against his lips.

"I know that. When are you going to do something about it and marry me?"

She turned away, taking evasive action. With a look of regret Richard helped himself to a drink, then went into the living room to talk with her father.

On Monday morning Nicole breezed into the newsroom and tossed the jacket to her outfit onto the back of her chair. One of her hands was shoving her white blouse into her skirt, while the other pushed her hair out of her way as she bent over to peruse the first edition of today's *Miami Guardian,* which was spread on her desk. She turned to the retraction printed on the inside page, wondering if the difficult-to-please Jake Slater would be satisfied now. She had come in on Saturday to prepare it, and Malcolm had gone over it with her, making sure it was worded so that it did not make her look like a reporter who hadn't done her homework but simply one who had made an unfortunate choice of words. The paper extended its apologies, citing Slater as South Florida's most efficient homicide detective. Malcolm saw that the piece was inserted in a strategic place guaranteed to be noticed by many. She and Malcolm figured that should leave a different impression in the minds of the public and smooth over Jake's ruffled feelings.

She stood there for a moment thinking of him again. It was not in a professional capacity that her mind was traveling. Instead it was hurtling like a runaway express train down a forbidden tunnel that was far, far more intriguing.

Chapter 2

At the end of the business day, Nicole left the imposing *Miami Guardian* building looking out over Biscayne Bay and turned toward the parking lot, the heels of her shoes clicking slowly over the pavement. The balmy Floridian breeze tossed her long chestnut hair against the side of her face. Raking it away again with her hand, she looked around the parking lot to locate her car. Every day she parked in a different place. Suddenly her gaze did a quick double take. The reason she had missed the car was all too clear. A tall broad-shouldered man, powerfully built yet leanly muscled, lounged against it, partially concealing it.

The man had an all-too-familiar face. It was Jake Slater. His silvered metallic-gray eyes traveled over her with unnerving thoroughness, making her blood run hot. Equally she surveyed him. He was wearing a gray suit that underscored his lethal good looks. As a concession to the heat of the day, his tie was loosened and his shirt collar unbuttoned.

Questions raced through her mind. What was he doing here? How did he know which car was hers? Malcolm's words danced into her mind, taunting her. *"Watch out for Jake. I think he's interested in you. He'll hunt you down and he'll pull you in."*

Reminding herself that absolutely, positively, under no circumstances was she having anything to do with a cop, she walked slowly forward. Under no circumstances would she go out with a dedicated detective. For many cops, their jobs became an obsession. Jake Slater had all the earmarks of one of those. The best ones paid dearly at the expense of their personal lives for their excellence. Nicole had firsthand knowledge of that. She had witnessed it while she was growing up, in her own parents' marriage. Mentally she steeled herself against his good looks, the quick, hard, dangerous charm and that resonant voice that stirred something deep inside her.

Wasting no more time, Jake pushed away from the side of the car. "How is my favorite female reporter?"

Words rolled off his tongue with a practiced sensual ease. Warning herself not to be beguiled, she couldn't help comparing those same words coming from Richard. From the pleased gleam in Jake's eyes, she guessed that he had seen the retraction in today's paper.

"So, you saw the retraction."

"That's right."

She quoted the insert. "N. Bradley of the *Miami Guardian* wishes to apologize . . . et cetera, et cetera."

The lean angularity of his face tapered into a hard male jaw. As she surveyed it slowly, the adrenaline started to flow, and her heart began to pound. What was it about him that made her want to take flight? The lazy smile that curved his mouth was sensual. When she looked into his eyes, the vital sexuality, the masculine innuendo came at her in drugging waves. No wonder he had crept into her mind over and over again.

Finally she found her voice again. "Is that why you're here, to tell me that you saw it?" she asked.

"Not the only reason..." She watched him drop a cigarette onto the ground and crush it beneath his foot. Every move he made was fluid and infinitely appealing to the eye. When he lifted his gaze, his eyes drilled into hers.

"I also wanted you to know that there are no hard feelings. Why don't we forget about the whole thing and have dinner together. I'd like to see you again." Once again she caught herself wanting to take him up on his invitation for dinner, but all her instincts warned her against it. Unable to reach for the door handle on the car, because he was standing directly in front of it, she was forced to look into his eyes.

"Are you serious?" The other night she had thought he was only trying to find out whether she was available. Once again she was bemused by his quicksilver approach.

"I've never been more serious about anything in my life."

"But only on Friday... I got the strongest impression you couldn't stand female reporters." Her hand reached out and he moved away from the side of the car, to allow her to unlock the door. But he stood un-nervingly nearby, watching her. Her hand shook slightly turning the key. He watched that, too.

"That was before you agreed to the retraction. Life is dynamic. Nothing stands still and nothing stays the same." The car door swung open and the heat inside hit her. She paused and looked up at him, not want-ing to slide in yet.

"You're not the sort of person who holds a grudge, are you?" She was beguiled by the complete turn-around. Her comment was both a statement and a question. She wanted him either to confirm or deny it.

His expression hardened for a fleeting moment. "That depends on what the grudge is about. There are some people I find pretty hard to forgive," he added.

"Well," she said, averting her gaze, "if you're no longer mad at me, then how do you feel now?" She knew she was flirting with him outrageously but she couldn't seem to stop herself. Everything about him goaded her on.

"Interested. I think I'm very interested. What about you?" The color of his eyes deepened again. A smile of teasing sensuality tugged at the corners of his mouth.

Every nerve ending in her being responded, but she shot him an apologetic look. "Sorry."

"Why sorry."

"Because I have to say I'm not interested."

"Liar." He laughed softly at her deception. Then his eyes narrowed. "You're interested all right. Just as interested as I am."

"You're very sure of yourself."

"I'm very sure about some things. This happens to be one of them."

"All right, I admit it. In a way you're right, but I still have to say I'm uninterested because of the way I feel. You're not my type."

Cynical amusement danced in his eyes. "Type? What do you mean, I'm not your type?" The tone of his voice challenged her. No such thing existed, his eyes said.

Sliding into the hot car, she put the key in the ignition. Her head angled to one side, she peered up at him. "Well, for one thing, you're not my type because you're a cop." Her look and tone implied there were other equally potent reasons. "I try to avoid detectives."

With one arm resting on the roof of the car he looked down at her. "Why is that?" His eyes narrowed slightly again. He seemed perplexed, but not offended.

"I like the sure thing. I want someone I can count on. That's what I'm aiming for. I like someone who turns up when he makes a date. Someone who arrives in one piece without bullet holes in him. Dedicated detectives are definitely unappealing to me and you look *very* dedicated, Detective Slater." She smiled to cover up the charged emotions that ran behind those words. He smiled back. Nicole got the distinct impression her remarks were having about the same effect as water running off a rock.

Lowering his head, he added some thoughts of his own. "You know something, Sunshine? One day, you're going to discover something really important."

"Oh, really. What's that?" She tried to look bored.

"Life is full of surprises. Nothing is more surprising than the way people are put together. They don't come neatly wrapped in *types*. They're fascinating mixtures." His voice lowered and his eyes darkened with meaning. "Sometimes the most unlikely mixtures meet. Things happen."

For a moment Nicole was so mesmerized, she was barely aware of the evening breeze caressing her face. An inner tremor shook her, until she felt a flush creeping over her entire body. The pull of his eyes held her riveted. Jake Slater had heart-stopping eyes. But it was his words that held her spellbound. Was he trying to tell her something about herself or himself? What was even more unnerving was that she sensed every inch of him was aware of the effect he was having on her. This potent attraction he triggered inside her made her feel intensely vulnerable and intensely feminine. Quickly, she threw another obstacle in his path.

"There's another reason."

"What's that?"

"I've been seeing someone for some time. We have an understanding, more or less." She started to pull the car door closed as if that ended things between them, but he clamped a hand on it, keeping it open.

"I don't want to alarm you or anything like that, but something tells me we'll be running into each other again. Somehow I don't think it's going to make any difference that you don't want to get involved with a detective, or that you have an understanding with someone...more or less." Riddled with hard-edged amusement, his gaze locked with hers as he rammed that observation home. Then he pulled back and slammed the car door shut with reverberating force.

Without looking at him again she twisted the key in the ignition. Eager to get out of the parking lot, she drove off at a fast clip. She stopped at the exit, looking left, then right, waiting for a gap in the traffic. Clamping and unclamping her fingers impatiently on the wheel, she glanced furtively in the rearview mirror. He was still standing there watching. Undeniably rattled, she realized there was something inside her that he tapped into that she hadn't known even existed. As soon as there was a break in the cars passing by, she shot out, joining the mainstream of traffic. It was as if she couldn't get away fast enough.

Jake Slater watched pensively as Nicole's car merged with the traffic. Life was full of surprises, all right. Just when you thought things were getting dull, life had a way of springing something gut-wrenching on you, dropping it right in your lap, and then saying, *Okay—what are you going to do about that?* What *was* he going to do about that—about that long-legged beauty who thumbed her nose at him every chance she got? Turning around slowly, he strode to his own car. His mind went shooting back in time to something he preferred not to think about. But meeting Mike Bradley's daughter had dragged it all up again and with it all the powerful underlying dark emotions that went with it. He reached into his pocket for a cigarette, wondering what in hell he was going to do about it. Ever since he met her in Oscar's Friday night with Malcolm Rogers, he'd known something was going to happen between them, because he had every intention of making it happen. Plans had been fermenting in his mind like some dark yeast from the moment he realized who she was. The wheels of his mind had been turning relentlessly toward a goal. But he wasn't sure exactly what steps he was going to take to achieve it...yet. There was one thing he was very sure about, though, and he was decent enough for it to make him a little uneasy. He was attracted to Nicole Bradley like no other woman he had ever met, but *for all the wrong reasons.*

The front door slammed. Nicole was in the kitchen tossing a green salad, Jake Slater's words still echoing inside her head. She heard her father sink into a chair and switch on the television to watch the evening news. Taking some Bolognese sauce out of the freezer, she put it into the microwave to thaw and reheat it, then drained the pasta, which was finished cooking. Suddenly her father's large, powerful frame filled the kitchen doorway.

"What's for dinner?"

"You could try saying hello," she shot back.

"Hello, what's for dinner."

"Spaghetti Bolognese." His face took on a pleased expression. She wasn't surprised—the dish was one of his favorites. "It will be ready in another few minutes."

He disappeared again to finish watching the news. While she waited for the sauce to heat she wondered why someone like herself, someone who liked to project a modern, career-minded image to the world, was still living with her father, still cooking for him. She was hardly the domestic type; she had convinced herself of that over and over again. She flicked her long hair away from her face in a gesture that was characteristic when she was setting her mind to something.

One of these days she was going to move out. But when? She had always told herself she was moving to a place of her own. She frowned at her ambivalence. It really was ridiculous that she was still cooking dinner for her father. All he had to do was roll one of those wounded looks across his face and she ended up cooking him another meal. Part of her wanted to put this whole world behind her. Yet part of her clung to it, somehow unable to let go. What made her stay? Was it just conditioning, or was it more than that? She had always thought she would marry out of this world, but then why didn't she leap at the chance to marry Richard? She wasn't going to be tradition bound, stuck in the past like a fly in amber. She wasn't going to get stuck in a cop's world where cops socialized together, intermarried and even bought houses in the same neighborhoods. God, there were whole enclaves populated almost solely by police officers. She had always told herself she was getting out of all this. Then why was she still here? her inner voice jeered again.

Sometimes she felt her emotions were playing a game of Ping-Pong, bouncing back and forth between what she told herself she wanted and what she actually did want. She leaned back against the kitchen counter, feeling suddenly weary. The words *fascinating mixtures* floated into her mind. She mulled them over. They were Jake Slater's words, describing people. She remembered the look in his eye when he uttered those words. He had said people didn't come neatly wrapped in types.

A few minutes later she called her father and placed the steaming plate of pasta in front of him. She watched him reach for the Parmesan cheese and sprinkle a generous amount onto the sauce-topped spaghetti. She placed the green salad at the side of his plate along with salad dressing.

While her father began to eat heartily, she walked to the freezer, reaching inside to get out the dessert. She stood there, absentmindedly spooning frozen yogurt into a dish. The scene in the parking lot ran through her mind again. Jake Slater leaning his hand on the car door, staring at her through the window. With the heat of the day intensified by the heat of the moment, it was a searing memory. Remembering how he had asked her if she was related to Mike Bradley when they first met, Nicole experienced a strong urge to find out what her father thought of him. She valued her father's opinion of people, since he was a pretty shrewd judge of character. Swinging herself around slowly with the frozen yogurt still in her hand, she broached the subject with a little half smile on her mouth. Her father was twirling some spaghetti on a fork, oblivious to the expression on his daughter's face.

"Someone I met recently says he knows you. Or, I should say he asked if I was your daughter." Her father lifted his gaze from his pasta just as he had completed twirling the strands around his fork. Nicole leaned back against the refrigerator door, letting her weight push it closed.

"Who was that?"

"Jake Slater."

The fork in her father's hand stilled in midair. In fact everything about him stilled. Slowly he put the pasta-laden fork down. A strange look appeared in his eyes, one that she couldn't identify readily. There was a bleakness in his eyes as if he were remembering something.

"I know Jake Slater. What about him? How do you know him?"

"I wrote a series on the tougher recruiting practices in the police force that had been implemented to offset previous incidents of corruption. I alluded to Slater as one of the new breed, better educated, with a better developed sense of values but still deadly accurate at his job."

"I read part of it. It was good. The guys in the department said on the whole it was a good series. What about Jake Slater?" her father prompted impatiently.

"In the series I referred to him as South Florida's deadliest cop. He didn't like it. He came to talk to Malcolm in Oscar's Lounge and I happened to be there. When he found out I had written it he demanded a retraction. That was how he discovered you were my father."

"Then what?"

"After the retraction was printed, he said there were no hard feelings and he asked me out to dinner."

"What did you say?" Her father's blue eyes quizzed her.

"I turned him down." She shrugged as if the incident had been of little importance. Her father's face mirrored intense relief.

"I'm glad to hear that. Stay away from him, Nicole. I don't like him."

"What have you got against Jake Slater?" She had never seen her father act this way about anyone before. Not quite this way. She watched his face grow taut.

"I don't like him, Nicole," he repeated, and she sensed he was searching his mind for some reasons that would satisfy her. "They've brought charges against him on several occasions."

"But they never made any stick."

"I want you to stay away from him. He's bad news." Her father's features hardened with growing agitation as she attempted to draw him out. His reaction both puzzled and surprised her. She thought Slater was a lot of things: arrogant, overbearingly confident and full of lethal charm when it came to women, but she knew he wasn't a bad cop. He had a sterling reputation when it came to executing his job. Usually that won her father's approval. She crossed the kitchen and sat down opposite him.

"There must be some reason for you to dislike him so?" With his head down her father looked as though he was concentrating on the pasta. He twirled it round and round on his fork. She saw a telltale muscle flick in his jaw. When he lifted his gaze, he exploded.

"I just told you I didn't like him. Do I have to draw you a picture?" The vehemence in his voice startled her. Her father was not a man who minced words; he was often blunt but he seldom lashed out at her like this. He paused. Seeing the stunned expression on her face, he softened his words. "I just don't like him. Call it a gut instinct. Slater is too smart for his own good. All right, he's a first-rate homicide detective. I'll give him that, but I don't want you to have anything to do with him."

Something inside Nicole rebelled. It was one thing for her father to offer an opinion saying he didn't care for someone, but it was quite another when he started telling her who she could see and who she couldn't. Silently she considered him for a moment, thinking it was a good thing she had already made up her mind not to have anything to do with Jake.

"Dad, you don't have to worry. I would never get involved with a detective. You know how I feel about cops."

Her father dropped his gaze for a moment when she said that. She knew he understood her. It was one of the reasons he wanted her to marry Richard, she supposed. Her father's own marriage had suffered considerably from his dedication to his job.

"All right, if that's the case." His reply shot across the kitchen swift and low. "When are you going to marry Richard? That's what I want to know." There was a look that suggested she would be safely out of harm's way when she married Richard. All would be well, some perfect world would materialize. Why hadn't she snapped it up, this perfect world? It was a testing remark. Somehow she felt backed into a corner where she didn't want to be. She didn't want to get involved with a cop and yet she didn't want to commit to Richard. The dizzying sensation that she was on some kind of emotional seesaw attacked her again.

"Stop pushing, and maybe I will," she murmured. He looked at her with a wry twist to his mouth and poured milk into his coffee.

When Nicole was alone that night in her room getting ready for bed, her father's words came back to her again. *When are you going to marry Richard?* But instead she thought of Jake Slater's steady eyes. The manly way he looked at her made her blood run hot. She told herself that he was intensely attractive but only in a purely physical way. It was normal to think about a man like that. Even if she never acted on any of those thoughts, they were to be expected, she told herself and then fell into a deep exhausted sleep.

Inside the Flamingo Express dance club, music exploded in Nicole's ears. The club was crowded. The dull roar of human voices competing with the loud music, shot through with laughter, made the atmosphere electric and slightly deafening. Nicole wanted nothing more than to dance the night away, not to think, not to feel, not to do much talking. All week long a restlessness she didn't want to put a name to had gripped her.

Richard's hand clasped hers. "Let's get a drink first." He led her through the crush of people to the bar to order some drinks, since getting a table looked hopeless for the moment. Near the bar people converged three and four deep. While they waited to get closer to the bar, Nicole's gaze wandered aimlessly around the noisy club. After a while she caught herself watching two men who had just entered.

With their backs facing her, she saw them stop to talk to the manager. There was something vaguely familiar about one of the men. People on the dance floor blocked her view but occasionally a gap appeared. Furtively she peered through the gaps. When she saw the glint of a bronze badge flash at the manager, her full powers of concentration came instantly into play. The tall man with his broad-shouldered back to her angled his head downward to talk to the manager, compensating for his superior height with that outwardly relaxed yet sharp-edged air of concentration. It was a characteristic, one of many that had become achingly familiar to her. When he turned slightly, her eyes confirmed what every nerve ending in her body had already relayed to her brain.

A sensual heat flooded her body. She realized how her mind had absorbed every detail about him like a sponge. Everything had stuck, every nuance of movement, every mannerism, every physical detail. Being confronted with them again only brought home the strong impression he had made on all her senses. The nameless longing that leaped inside her was now undeniable, explaining the restlessness that tormented her. Averting her head, she closed her eyes for a moment against the heady truth. She was attracted to Jake Slater like no man she had ever met before. Of all the people in the world why did it have to be him?

Jake and his partner were now questioning the bartender, probably checking out a lead. He was working late, she thought scornfully. The *dedicated* detective in action. Awakened desire curdled inside her. She turned away. Forget him, her inner voice warned.

Trained to be sharply observant, Jake swung his restless gaze around the club, that sixth sense coming into play like the fine tuning on a stereo. Nicole felt a telltale warmth invading her skin. She slipped between two people, trying to merge with the crowd at the bar. But Richard had managed to get near the bar and signaled the bartender. The sudden movement caught Jake's sharp eye. When Richard moved closer to the bar, a gap opened up. Alarm shot through her as Jake turned completely around. Unerringly he spotted her immediately. The radar between them was set on high frequency. Nicole stood poised for flight.

Handsome, hypnotic and powerful, he stood motionless, like a man deciding what he was going to do about it. He stared at her, his silvered eyes executing a stinging sensation. Pretending not to see him, she leaned over with an air of intimacy to say something to Richard, whose eyes were on the bartender mixing their drinks.

Turning back to her, Richard welcomed her attention, making some comment about the concert they had been to. Nicole heard herself responding but she wasn't sure of what she was saying. All she knew was that a strange pounding excitement was coursing through her as Jake shouldered his way through the crowd toward them. She knew that without looking. Every instinct in her body told her so. She was too acutely aware of Jake's compelling presence to concentrate fully on anything else. The crowd parted. Nicole looked up, flicking away her hair in that characteristic gesture that was both provocative and an indication that she was on edge. Jake loomed over them. The daring, reckless glint in his eyes acknowledged her presence.

"Nicole."

Simultaneously Richard turned around and handed Nicole a drink. Jake wasted no time, introducing himself and explaining his intrusion. "I'm Jake Slater from Homicide."

From beneath thick lashes, Nicole watched Richard's hand shoot out to clasp Jake's. Struggling to stop the mad pounding of her heart, she made a valiant effort to compose herself while the two men greeted each other. It gave her some valuable breathing space. An amiable look slid across Richard's face, as the two men acknowledged each other. They worked on the same team, both on the side of law and justice. The greeting was man to man, profession to profession. Nicole wondered what Jake wanted.

"I've seen you in court, haven't I? Giving evidence on the Ramirez case?" Richard inquired.

"That's right. Nicole and I know each other from the work she did on the series on the Miami Police Department." His gaze slid to her face momentarily with that fixed look of absorption she had noted the day he walked into Oscar's Bar and Lounge. He was after something.

"I want to ask her a few questions. Could I borrow her for a few minutes?"

"Sure, why not. Anything to aid the cause of justice," Richard responded with an air of bonhomie. Forcing a smile to her face, Nicole followed Jake. She didn't know where they were going. She put one foot in front of the other, sensing him studying her from under three-quarter-closed eyes. It wasn't the cause of justice that was behind that veiled expression in those heart-stopping eyes. She didn't want to talk to him and he knew it, but it was better to dance one dance with him and find out what he wanted.

His hand propelled her in front of him, resting possessively on her waist. She felt like a slave girl being marched to the block. The forced smile on her lips vanished as they moved deeper and deeper into the crowd on the dance floor so they were completely obscured from Richard's sight. Reaching the center she turned around and confronted Jake.

"What's this all about? What do you want?"

"What do you think I want?" Daring, reckless, compelling, he stood towering over her. A lazy smile crept across his face.

"You might as well wipe that smile off your face. You're wasting your time. I'm with him, in case you hadn't noticed." The silent message in her eyes was clear. It meant now and from now on. She glanced uneasily around her. The gyrating bodies of those around them edged Nicole closer to the powerful man in front of her. There was no way out. Eyes that glittered with experience took in the off-the-shoulder black dress, the tantalizing cleavage exposed and the way the fabric clung lovingly to each curve.

"The dress, I like it." Lowering his head, he breathed the words against the side of her face. Suddenly someone backed into Nicole, thrusting her into Jake's arms forcefully. He caught her, his hands locked firmly on her hips. A flash of something inexplicable curled deep within her.

"Aren't you supposed to be working or something? I saw you flash a badge. The dedicated cop isn't actually having a night off, is he?" she taunted, trying to offset the way he made her feel and the dangerous look in his eyes.

"One of these days I'm going to do something about that smart mouth." Speaking the words close to her ear so that he could make himself heard, he took her arms and locked them around his neck, making her feel like some gauche teenager who had to be taught the rudiments of making out. He had the advantage of taking her by surprise. No one had ever treated her like this before. "You asked my why I'm here. I'm here following up a very hot lead. Are you going to cooperate and help me with my inquiries?" he teased mercilessly.

She could see that he was enjoying himself immensely at her expense. Her eyes continued to scan his steadily. Finally she found her voice again.

"This hot lead you're following up. It's a dead end."

"I think it has lots of potential myself," he observed, narrowing his eyes on her mouth.

"You're wasting your time. You don't want a pushy female reporter." Mulling it over in her mind, she came up with an easy solution to his quest. "What you want is one of those nice quiet types. Someone who will sit at home waiting for you to get your head blown off. That's what I see you with. Someone you can tell what to do. Someone who will say 'yes, darling,' 'no, darling,' 'whatever you say, dear.' That's not me."

Her words didn't deter him. They only made him laugh deep in his throat.

"I don't see myself with one of those nice, quiet types. I see myself with a long-legged female reporter with a smart mouth and green eyes. She keeps holding me off and all it does is make me want her more."

It was the age-old message, the unmistakable masculine invitation. Wagging her head slowly from side to side with mock regret, but deliberately tormenting him, she retorted easily, "But you don't like female reporters and I don't want to get involved with a cop. Remember?"

"It's the woman inside the reporter that interests me." He breathed the words slowly into her ear, while his hand trailed slowly down the hollow of her spine in her bare back, emphasizing his words. Needles of longing crawled down her arms and legs, telltale sensations of her unequivocal response to his raw masculinity. When his hand reached the lower part of her back he pressed her intimately into him. There was no longer any pretense of dancing. Their feet weren't moving.

"Are you going to deny what we're feeling right now?" His low-pitched voice coiled around her. Her hands tightened around his neck. She pressed her face against the side of his, inhaling the warm male scent of him, trying to still the sensations he aroused, fighting them.

"Why are you doing this? It's not fair."

"What's not fair? The way you make me feel isn't fair. The way I can't stop thinking about you, that's not fair either."

Her eyes closed for a moment. She decided to concede some ground, since nothing else was working. "All right. Maybe there is some kind of strong physical attraction between us. But that doesn't mean we have to do anything about it."

His lips grazed the shell of her ear again. "There's no question about it, Nicole. There's more than some kind of physical attraction between us. Believe me when I say that. Why don't you give the man behind the badge a chance? Look behind the cop. Why don't you get to know me?"

She shifted her head and looked straight into his eyes. "I don't want to get to know you." The husky tremor in her voice and the look in her eyes told him she was a liar. Her whole being wanted to do that very thing.

"What are you going to do? Go on seeing that stiff-necked lawyer?" He indicated, with a flick of his head the general direction where Richard was sitting at a table. "Is that the sure thing you were talking about?"

"Yes," she flared. "He's the type of man I want to marry someday."

His features hardened at her response. A steeliness invaded his eyes. Ignoring her comments, he said, "Let's forget about Richard for a minute. Let's go somewhere where we can hear ourselves talk." Without waiting for her reply he propelled her toward a dark corner away from the dance floor. Off the beaten path the music faded slightly. Knowing she shouldn't allow him to plead his case, she found herself doing exactly that. Leaning indolently against the wall, Nicole wondered what was happening to her. With one hand planted firmly above her head, Jake bent his head to make up for the disparity in their height, much as she had seen him do when talking to the manager. But now the full impact of his eyes was focused unwaveringly on her. All his attention was directed at her. Week-kneed she listened, knowing what one of his prime suspects must feel like. He probably excelled at breaking them down. First winning their confidence, then softening them up and finally moving in for the kill.

"Let's think about me and you for a minute. What has it been like since you first met me? Do you catch yourself thinking about me off and on?" Lifting his hand, he caught her jaw, forcing her to look straight into his eyes when she answered. Silently she saw that look of earthy sensuality creeping into his. Why was she so attracted to him? The answer eluded her.

"Do you find yourself arguing inside your head with yourself, telling yourself all the reasons why you're not interested in me, why you won't get involved with me?"

"Maybe once or twice." The reluctant admission was finally dragged from her.

"Only once or twice, Nicole?" His eyes challenged hers. He wouldn't let her avert her gaze, his hand still held her jaw. "Do you ever ask yourself why you keep telling yourself that you're not interested?"

"No. I never get that far."

"I'll bet you haven't. You know why, don't you?"

"No," she whispered.

"Liar." He laughed softly. "I can see it in your eyes. I'm no fool, Nicole. I'm experienced enough to know when a woman wants me." Her face flamed at his words. Like a hound on the scent of blood, he had her cornered. "You've got that bruised, bemused look in your eyes. The smart, hotshot reporter doesn't know what's hit her. You're just as interested in me as I am in you. I can't get you out of my head, any more than you can get me out of yours. Doesn't that sound more like the truth than what you've been telling yourself about Richard? What are we going to do about it?"

"Nothing," she snapped. "Just leave me alone. I'm not letting any dedicated cop into my life. I've seen firsthand the damage dedication to the force can do to a relationship." Shaking her head negatively, as if she could make it all go away, she knew deep in her heart what he said was true. She did have to keep telling

herself over and over again she wasn't interested in
him, when all the time she couldn't get him out of her
head. In their brief but heady acquaintance he had
aroused something inside her that Richard had never
aroused. And she did have to keep telling herself that
she didn't want it, that nameless thing she didn't want
to put a name to. He was confusing her, muddling her
mind and moving far too fast.

"I'm not going to let hormones rule my life," she
asserted in a shaky voice, looking steadily into his eyes
again. A glimmer of satisfaction surfaced in Jake's
eyes.

"What are you saying? Doesn't your friend over
there turn you on? What's he like in bed? If you ever
got that far."

"You know something. You're too damned blunt."
She reached up to shove his hand away from her jaw,
but it remained firmly planted there.

"Richard happens to be a gentleman. That's more
than I can say for you," she added softly.

"All right, maybe I'm no gentleman. But I know
something about you. You must have a pretty good
idea of what life with Richard is going to be. Is that
what you want?"

"It's better than having no life with someone who's
never there or someone who doesn't come home at all.
I told you how I felt about cops. I grew up surrounded by them. I know what their world is like, and
it's a world I want no part of. Stay away from me."
Her passionate temper was ripped loose from its nice
comfortable moorings. The wild streak she kept so
carefully hidden was surfacing with a vengeance. Jake

knew exactly what to say to get to her. With unerring ease he had struck a raw nerve.

"How long have you been going out with him?" he continued with grim male relentlessness. "How long have you been lying to yourself?"

"It's none of your business. Don't you realize we're crazy to be having this conversation at all!"

"It's easy controlling him—isn't it. But what about me?" She flashed a potent warning at him with her eyes, but he ignored it. "It's not so easy with me."

"Shut up." Her breathing was agitated and uneven. Her legs had developed a strange kind of tremor.

"I bother you like hell, don't I? I'll tell you another thing you don't like about me, besides my being a cop. You know you can't control me. But you keep wondering what it would be like with me. You're curious. You want me but that scares the hell out of you, too. You're not willing to pay the price, are you?"

"Getting involved with you would be like a roller coaster ride, full of thrills. But what happens when the wild ride is over and the thrill is gone?"

His heart-stopping eyes honed in on her mouth. "I haven't got the time to go into that with you now, Nicole. Maybe later when we get to know each other better. But I want a lot more than cheap thrills." In the dark corner of the noisy club she could barely make out the contours of his face, but his eyes were intent and serious. Mesmerized, she couldn't shake the feeling that he meant what he said. This was no casual line. But what exactly did he mean?

"When you're out with Richard, here's something else for you to rationalize away." When he pulled her in his arms, the struggle was brief. A rough male ten-

derness emanated from him as if he realized he had
pushed her too hard. All her defenses were down.
With a choked sob of surrender her mouth met his. He
cupped her face between his hands, teasing her mouth
with his.

"Give in to me, Nicole." He breathed the soft
command against her lips.

"You're everything I loathe," she protested softly.

"Maybe I'm everything you *think* you loathe," he
retorted. "Maybe I'm really everything you want."

Her body shuddered in response. Then his mouth
found hers in the dark, claiming hers with a fiery possession. Raw and urgent, his compelling, ruthless
brand of sensuality took over. The driving force of his
kiss pinned her to the wall, arching her spine and
molding her hips to his hard thighs. With a soft moan
of discovery her mouth mated with his. Her hands slid
inside his jacket around the leanly muscled contours
of his broad back. Everything in the loud noisy club
faded into oblivion. Engulfed in a sensually charged
storm, she felt Jake's animal warmth pulsate into her
body in waves. The thrust of his hips, the long hard
line of his legs invaded her soft curves and his hands
locked on her hips. He deepened the full-blown passionate kiss, molding her intimately against him. A
fervor consumed them. Nicole strained in to him,
wanting more, wanting his hands all over her. Without realizing what she was doing, she locked her arms
around his neck. Pressing into him sensuously, she
goaded him on, until his breathing was labored and
she felt him growing hard against her thigh. The fire
was in danger of blazing out of control because they
both wanted more.

Breaking off the kiss he turned his head to one side. He whispered roughly against her ear, still holding her locked against him with hard determined hands. "Want me?" His hand covered hers, guiding it down to his thigh. "I sure as hell want you."

Everything but the raw longing had faded from her mind. She pressed her lips against the side of his face, knowing she should plead with him to stop, but she wanted him to go on. Her wild heart ruled. She moaned softly, leaving him in no doubt as to what she felt. He had gotten the unequivocal response he was looking for, the one his experience told him he would get. But she sensed that maybe he had gotten more than he bargained for.

Mercifully he broke off the steamy exchange. Holding her away, he gazed down at her, reining in his own desire, but it was costing him. She felt a delirious satisfaction that she affected him as strongly as he affected her. Desire silvered his eyes. She met his gaze in wondering silence. When at last he released her, she was agitated and flushed, feeling humiliated by her own behavior. With a disturbed look in her eyes, she used the only weapon she had left.

"I told you," she breathed shakily, as if it were her last dying breath, "I'm not getting involved with any cop."

"Maybe we are already involved, whether you like it or not." The words shot across the space between them, low and quick. The truth of his words seared her mind. She could never have responded to him the way she just had if there wasn't already some kind of emotional involvement. But she didn't thank him for pointing it out to her.

For a moment she stared at him numbly. Suddenly her soft mouth curved into a mutinous little twist. Her hand shot out to slap away that insinuating look in his eyes. The stinging physical rebuke had little effect. His head barely moved. But he seized the offending hand with lightning reflexes. Sizzling silence prevailed.

"Maybe that will give you something to rationalize away, too," she whispered softly.

"Don't ever do that again, because so help me, next time I'll make you pay for it." His low-pitched tone warned her, leaving her in no doubt that he meant every word. While she still had some self-possession left she turned and walked away. Her blood was molten, her heart was throbbing and her legs felt as if they might not carry her. She escaped hurriedly into the rest room to repair the damage. Once inside she leaned against the wall, staring into the mirror. There was accusation in her eyes. She covered her face with one hand.

Chapter 3

You fool! How could you have let him kiss you like that? How could you have responded like that? The sensual attack left her humiliated as well as frustrated. She stood with her eyes closed, trying to calm down, striving for control, and trying to still the shaking inside. Finally, when she felt she had achieved some degree of calmness, she opened her eyes. With a shaky hand she smoothed her hair where his hand had been. Sensations persisted. Her lips felt bruised. She still tasted him on her lips. The clean male scent of him lingered in her mind. The imprint of his hand on her lower back pressing her into him urgently, intimately, left a rubbery sensation in her legs.

Turning away from the mirror, she composed herself and walked out of the rest room. She made her way back through the crush of people, glancing furtively around. But she couldn't see Jake anywhere.

Relief and disappointment mingled inside her. When she returned to the table she forced a smile to her face.

Richard looked up at her. "I thought you had gotten lost."

"Would you mind if we left now?"

"What happened to Jake Slater? I lost sight of you both on that crowded floor."

"Oh, him?"

"Yeah, him," Richard said dryly.

"He had to leave. I slipped into the rest room for a few minutes. I'm sorry to have taken so long."

"Did he upset you, Nicole?"

"Upset me?" she echoed distantly with a questioning frown. She felt as though she were on some elevated plane and still had to come down to earth. "No. What makes you think that?"

Richard shot her a peculiar look. "There's a look in your eyes. Are you feeling all right?" He laughed softly.

At precisely this moment Nicole was finding it hard to see the funny side of anything. She knew only one thing that was remotely funny. Jake had made a fool out of her with such ease it was laughable. Only she wasn't laughing. Instead she hoped fervently that he had proved whatever silly notion his male ego needed to prove, and she also hoped his face stung where her hand had struck him. She looked at Richard again.

"I'm feeling all right, just a little tired." If he didn't stop looking at her that way she was going to scream.

"Well, I guess we'd better be going. I've got an early start tomorrow, too. There's no point in dragging out the evening." Richard signaled the waiter for the bill.

She watched him in taut silence, her mind still trying to come to terms with what had happened. In those few moments, a man she hardly knew had reduced her to such a state that, had he asked her to go with him to finish what they had started, she would no doubt have said yes. It was incomprehensible. She had kissed him back with a wildness and abandon she hadn't known was inside her. It was humiliating. And she knew he had done it on purpose just to show her the power he wielded.

When Nicole got home she slammed the front door without thinking. Leaning against it, she knew she was more irritated with herself than with Jake Slater. She closed her eyes, trying to blot out the images her mind kept replaying.

"What's all that racket?" her father grumbled as he emerged from his room. He stood glowering at her with a questioning look in his eyes. He was in his undershirt and pants and barefoot. She looked up with a guilty start.

"I'm sorry. I didn't realize I was being so noisy."

"You look mad about something," he remarked, eyeing her suspiciously. "Did you have some kind of blowup with Richard?"

"No, I...uh—" She moved away from the door, avoiding his eyes. Her mind raced to come up with a quick excuse. "We just couldn't agree on where to go. It was childish of us, and we got into a silly, petty argument. We were tired, that was all. We should have both stayed at home." Her words seemed to jeer at her. She certainly should have stayed home, she thought.

"Humph." He disappeared back into his room. Not for a minute did he believe her, she knew. She never could put anything over on him. Nicole walked slowly into her own bedroom. Throwing her handbag onto a chair, she walked over to the dresser and started un-zipping her dress. She shed her clothes, still locked in a trance brought on by those moments of sensual magic with Jake in the dark corner of the nightclub. The few moments they had been together, the way she had felt in his arms, were burned into her mind irre-vocably. She doubted whether she would ever be able to forget it. Especially branded into her mind was the knowing look in his eyes, and the way he seemed able to see inside her. His shrewd insight and his words about what was happening between them echoed in her mind over and over.

But even more seductive than the strong come-on was the fact that she admired him as a man. She felt compelled by him, in spite of the fact that he was in a profession that supposedly turned her off. In spite of the fact that her father didn't like him. He was intel-ligent, good at his job, and she instinctively felt that they would enjoy being together if she let her guard down. His whole personality, his male strength, had left a powerful indelible impression that she knew she was going to have a lot of trouble forgetting. It had totally engulfed her. The way his hand had captured her face. The way his mouth had taken hers with such firm possession. The kiss had been demanding, pul-sating with something wild and angry within him. No one had ever kissed her that way, no one had ever held her that way. No one had ever made her feel that way before.

Yet he had touched something deep inside her, too. That was the most disturbing part of meeting him again. That was the part she couldn't put from her mind. He hadn't just grabbed her in sheer lust—it was more complicated than that. She would bet her life on it. A fumbled, bungled kiss in the dark corner, she would have dismissed from her mind. Written it off as just one of those unpleasant situations one forgot about. But it hadn't been like that. Most people knew that where passion ruled, there were blind spots. Unconscious feelings that even the most oblivious people were unaware of and seemed to have little control over. That was what left her feeling so vulnerable. She was back on that emotional seesaw. No matter how much she told herself she didn't want to be attracted to him, she responded to him out of some deep-seated desire that his own desire had tapped into almost from the very beginning. They had been drawn together like opposite poles on a magnet, like interlocking fingers from opposite hands.

She switched out the light and tried to go to sleep but sleep was a long time coming. Her hand strayed to her lips where his had been, then dropped to her hip. She ran her fingers along the curve of it where his hand had molded her sensuously against him. Closing her eyes, she remembered how she had felt and shuddered under her own desire. She knew that she wanted to feel that way again.

When Jake left his partner that evening he stopped his car near the beach and started to walk down an isolated strip. It was his favorite place to think and he often came here for that reason, especially when something was bugging him about a difficult case. But tonight it was personal and had nothing to do with police work. The silver strand gleamed and disappeared into the distance. He lit a cigarette, irritated with himself for weakening. He studied the ember glow, trying to sort out his feelings for the young woman he had backed into a corner. He wanted her, all right, but he had known that from the beginning. He also knew he was no slouch where women were concerned and usually got what he went after. But he had pushed Nicole unusually hard. He had never pushed a woman like that before. He never had to. Because he had never before been in a position where so many mixed emotions were involved. As he stared out at the inky waters heaving in the darkness, the bleak aspect reminded him of a time he liked to forget. A time when Mike Bradley had loomed large in his life. He had been fifteen at the time, a kid, but he came away hating Mike Bradley like a man.

He could still see the scene in his mind. He had been spending the weekend with one of his friends, Mick Hauser. The weekend plans had gotten all fouled up when Mick had been rushed to the hospital for an emergency appendectomy. Leaving Mick's anxious parents hovering outside the operating room, Jake had hitched a ride home. Even in those days he had been restless by nature. He could never stay put in any one place for very long. Whipcord lean and six feet tall, Jake had almost reached his full height, but he hadn't filled out yet. When he eased quietly into the house on catlike strides, he had heard sounds coming from the bedroom that his mind didn't want to put a name to. They were not the sounds of a burglar or trespasser.

They were rhythmic sounds that could only be attributed to one activity. The thought that his father was away shot into his mind, making his skin crawl. But a sinister, compelling curiosity drove him on. When he pushed open the door to his parents' bedroom, the scene before him was burned into his mind irrevocably. Even now it triggered a searing raw reaction. A man was in bed with his mother. Her bare legs were visible. The raw, unbridled sounds of pleasure on her part instantly ruled out rape. But the rhythmic pumping of the man's lean flanks filled him with a white-hot rage. The next thing he remembered was hitting the man with everything he had. His sole intention was to kill him as quickly as possible. Somehow the man got him out of the room, and held him off, trying to reason with him. The next thing Jake remembered was hitting the streets. He never could remember where he went. A distilled, highly charged sensation that blotted out everything consumed him. For hours he wandered the streets with no destination in mind, not thinking of food or sleep or any of the things that normally occupied his mind. Flashbacks tormented him, playing over and over in his mind. So many illusions had been shattered, and he tried not to think at all. Only hatred for the man he would later identify as Mike Bradley remained.

When he finally returned home his mother had been hysterical with worry and remorse. Jake refused to speak to her. When his father returned from yet another business trip, he immediately sensed the trauma that had invaded his home and eventually pried out of his wife what had happened. His father's reaction had been typical. A man of rigid self-discipline and long

silences, he never referred to the incident openly again.
It was as if it had never happened. His mother broke
off the affair, but a few months later, either acciden-
tally or intentionally, she took an overdose of barbi-
turates. His father never remarried. Driven by his own
personal demons he had gone on to make a fortune in
real estate.

Jake knew that he had carried his hatred of Mike
Bradley buried deep inside him all these years. It had
lain dormant, undetected by the outside world. But it
had driven him, too. Who could ever have figured it
would surface again after all these years, bringing with
it to tempt him the perfect opportunity for revenge.
But that was exactly what had happened when Nicole
Bradley walked into his life. He felt himself yielding
to the temptation to use her to get back at her father.
It was driving him relentlessly to pursue her, helped by
the physical and mental attraction between them.

He no longer wanted to kill Mike Bradley, as he had
in his youth. Now he had a more subtle weapon of revenge. He was going to watch Bradley squirm with the
knowledge that Jake Slater wanted to get between his
daughter's legs. He wanted to make Mike sweat, and
sweat he would, because Jake knew that Nicole's father would never have told his daughter about the affair. No man in his right mind would, if he wanted to
hang on to his daughter's love and respect. Jake in-
tended to capitalize on Nicole's ignorance and let it
work for him. But how far was he willing to go? he
asked himself. His gaze narrowed on some distant invisible horizon.

There was only one catch to this whole situation. He
had discovered it to his surprise in that dark corner in

the club tonight. Underneath the brittle shell there was a softness, a vulnerability in Nicole that really got to him, much more than he cared to admit. She wasn't what he had first expected. This unexpected vulnerability brought out a protective streak in him, spawned a rough tenderness that he didn't know what to do with. Don't let emotions creep into this, he warned himself. Mike Bradley had this coming. No woman was going to mess up his mind.

Up until now he had never let emotions complicate his relationships with women. His treatment of women was cavalier at best, predatory more often. With one look he let them know what he wanted. Were they interested? a questioning gleam in his eyes would ask. If so, he moved in and took full advantage of the situation. When it was over he turned his back and walked away with few second thoughts but certainly no regrets. He liked that kind of arrangement. It suited him down to his fingertips. Satisfaction on both sides, no histrionics when it was over, no loose ends to clutter up his life. All neat and unemotional. He'd never thought anything was wrong with that, never questioned himself too closely about it, and he never bothered to analyze it. He had a blind spot. It was a mile wide and two feet thick and made him emotionally inaccessible to any woman. He had had affairs by the score, but no woman had gotten near his heart and he didn't see any reason for changing the status quo. He told himself he was happy with the way things stood, and he wasn't going to let any woman change that, especially not Mike Bradley's daughter.

He let his finger propel the half-smoked cigarette into the darkness. The glow careened into the black

sky, the rustle of the palms lining the beach obliterat-
ing the sound of the fiery tip hitting the water. He
turned and headed back to his car.

When Nicole emerged from the newspaper building the full heat of the late afternoon struck her.
Knowing the car would be like an oven again, she began peeling off the brief fitted jacket that matched her
slim skirt. Underneath she wore a white sleeveless top
that buttoned down the front. She released the top two
buttons and slung the jacket over her arm. Ominous
rumbling overhead indicated an impending storm. The
rainy season had arrived in South Florida. Every day,
often at the same time, there was a torrential downpour, not as heavy as the monsoons of the Far East,
but bringing them to mind all the same. Knowing the
heavens would open up any minute with the deluge,
she quickened her pace in the daily search for her car,
which she luckily spotted.

Jake was still on her mind. She'd thought about him
on and off since this morning; the result had been a
frustrating day, because her mind had been only half
on her work.

Suddenly the storm began and she was forced to run
the last one hundred yards or so. She slipped breathlessly into her car just in time to avoid getting soaked.
As she drove down the streets, the palm trees, whipped
by the gathering winds and torrential rain, resembled
wild hula dancers out of control. It was the rainy day
that brought back memories.

Her father had come home from the war in Vietnam on a rainy day just like this one, she recalled as
the windshield wipers struggled to keep up with the

sheets of rain. She remembered going to the airport as a small child with her mother in the drenching rain. Nicole remembered twirling around in a new dress and gleaming patent leather shoes, jumping up and down with excitement, admiring her mother with childlike eyes. Her mother had looked beautiful that day, turning heads everywhere. She was proud of her mother and even prouder of her father when she saw him striding across the tarmac toward them in his uniform decorated with medals.

First her father had embraced her mother, locking her in his arms. Nicole remembered gazing up at them as they strained in to each other with a strange fervor that mystified her. The two figures had looked twice as tall as they actually were, the way grown-ups always did to small children. Her father had practically lifted her mother off her feet. When the embrace ended he had caught sight of Nicole and lifted her high into the air over his head. They all laughed and talked easily together as they drove home to pick up the threads of everyday life.

The days had passed happily. A warm glow had suffused their lives; she never remembered seeing her mother happier. Nicole had watched her father and mother with their heads together bent over books, underneath the light hanging over the kitchen table. Her father had then passed at the top of his class and embarked on a new career, law enforcement. Looking back now, Nicole speculated that, coming home from Vietnam, conditioned by the adrenaline highs of two tours of duty, her father found that law enforcement offered a similar excitement in a way. Whatever it was that attracted him to the career, he excelled at it and moved swiftly up the promotion ladder into the plainclothes division.

As the years passed, Nicole noticed changes in the way her parents regarded each other. At first they were small changes, but as more and more time passed they grew more and more telling. Her mother's face changed, the softness went from it and some of the prettiness. There seemed to be fewer and fewer smiles and fewer and fewer happy times when they were together, until eventually there were none at all. Soon there seemed to be only raised voices and accusations hurled back and forth, accompanied by blistering remarks. Her father's low retorts were sharp and swift when he bothered to respond at all. His facial expression seemed permanently taut and stony. Late at night, raised voices coming from her parents' bedroom couldn't be ignored. On one occasion she remembered her father standing in the hallway shouting at her mother. "You're my wife, dammit." The slamming front door had reverberated through the silent house afterward, leaving only an alien silence.

Life had continued in this disturbing way until one day her father had come to the school and taken her home. She knew the minute she saw him that something was terribly, terribly wrong. His face was haggard and wore a closed-in expression. The hushed voices when she got home, the announcement that her mother had gone into the hospital, the crushing final announcement that her mother wasn't coming home at all, was like a metal door clanging shut in her mind. An embolism had been the cause of her death, but in Nicole's child's mind, it was something about her beloved daddy that had caused all the trouble.

These memories flashed before her now. It was the first time she had thought of them. Vaguely, at the back of her mind, they surfaced inexplicably from time to time, coloring her viewpoint and disturbing the even keel of her life. Then they often vanished just as quickly like mist from a moor when the sun came out. It was something over which she had no control. When her mind tried to come to grips with it, it eluded her, leaving only a faint sense of menace and a sensation of something irretrievably lost.

She swung her car into the driveway and switched off the engine. She sat there staring out at the rain, lost in thought. When she walked into the parking lot, Jake Slater had been so much on her mind that she'd half expected to see him waiting for her again, leaning indolently against her car. Relief had washed over when he was not there; he was the last person on earth she wanted to see today. Last night was still all too fresh in her mind. Vivid pictures tormented her once again, reminding her that she had gone a little crazy. Nicole propped her elbow on the steering wheel and rested her face in the palm of her hand, vaguely aware that the rain was slowing down.

"Damn you," she whispered in anguish. "Damn you for getting inside me." She wondered if Jake had any real feelings at all. Was he nothing but an opportunist, a hunter who enjoyed the chase?

"No," she whispered. He was much more than that. For all his hard-edged sensuality and masculine aggressiveness she sensed he had feelings. But what was at their source?

Chapter 4

When she got inside, the silence of the house palled. She walked over to the bookshelves, switched on the compact disc player, and music instantly filled the room.

Some time later she emerged barefoot from the bathroom, having just showered. A white towel turban cocooned her hair and her floor-length terry-cloth robe was wrapped around her wet body. The doorbell began buzzing insistently and repeatedly as if someone was leaning on it. Hastily she tied the sash to her robe tighter, and then went to answer the door.

Who was that? Of all the times for someone to be leaning on the doorbell, it would be now. She knew it wasn't Richard; he had called her at work that afternoon to tell her he had to cancel their usual Friday night dinner date. He had to go out of town to get a deposition and was probably on his way to Ohio by

now. Her father had his key, and even if he had left it
somewhere she knew he would never be back this
early. On Friday nights he usually stayed out until the
early hours of the morning. When she yanked open
the door, her eyes widened with disbelief.

Filling the doorway with his presence was Jake
Slater. With the unhurried movements of a man trying to make up his mind about something, he dropped
a cigarette to the ground, crushing it pensively beneath his foot.

"Well, aren't you going to invite me in?"

"I'm not sure that I should," she retorted softly.

"What would you say if I told you I came over to
apologize, to tell you that maybe I was out of line last
night?"

The sensual glint in Jake's heart-stopping eyes made
his words highly suspect. He looked about as repen-
tant as a tomcat intent on consuming a canary. Folding her arms in front of her, Nicole leaned back
indolently against the doorjamb, letting her gaze slide
over his face. "How did you find out where I live?"

"I'm a detective, remember?"

"I remember, all right." She started to push the
door closed in his face as if she could push him out of
her life forever. But with the same lightning reflexes
that she remembered from the first time she met him,
he blocked the movement, as if it were child's play.
There was a kind of inevitability about him that de-
fied any logic.

"You know you can't get rid of me that easily. And
I know that you don't want me to go."

His gaze pointedly dropped to the front of her gaping robe. As if it were some kind of invitation. With a

quick movement, her hand pulled the neckline of her robe closed. Barefoot and with very little on underneath, she knew he had the psychological advantage. But he was on her territory, so she did at least have that. A surly man could always be ordered out of the house, she reassured herself.

"Since you're here, and since you're already halfway in the door, you might as well come in."

Amusement glittered in his eyes as he followed her inside like a lion stalking some long-legged bird of prey. Nicole walked in front of him, past an atrium filled with a jungle of exotic growth that occupied one wall of the living room.

"Have a seat—make yourself at home. You will anyway."

Jake shot a wary, restless look around the room. Her gaze followed his. The room was a soothing shade of pale green, with a matching carpet and furnished with contemporary pieces. An overstuffed sofa with loose cushions flanked one wall, a fireplace with two fireside chairs in mustard completed the seating arrangement. Built-in shelves and tables and brass lamps dotted the room, which was a sanctum of peace and calm.

"Where's the old man?"

"If you mean my father," she said, "he goes out with his friends on Friday nights."

"Friends? You mean his men friends, or his girlfriend?" Jake shot back laconically. There was a bitter tinge to his tone that she didn't understand.

"He doesn't have a girlfriend. What are you doing here?" she asked.

"I told you I came to apologize. I was out of line last night, and I want to make it up to you. Have you had any dinner yet?"

"No."

"I haven't eaten, either. Why don't we go out for something?"

She didn't answer. She just stood looking steadily back at him. One part of her brain was wondering why she was allowing this to happen. The other part watched in bewildered confusion.

"It's more than your life is worth to admit that you might like to have dinner with me. Isn't it?" he taunted softly.

A telltale warmth invaded her skin. His words echoed the truth. She felt paralyzed, held prisoner. He overshadowed her. His pinning gaze lifted slowly to the towel turban around her hair. Without warning his hand seized the towel, pulling it from her head. Her body flinched. Her rich hair cascaded around her face. She dragged in a shaky breath, because somehow the gesture was deeply erotic. Almost as if he had stripped away some vital piece of clothing.

"You're beautiful," he said quietly. "Did I get around to telling you that yet?" He sounded as if his discovery was made with an extreme reluctance on his part. For a moment his whole attitude seemed abstracted by it. Then he quickly recovered.

"Get dressed. We'll go somewhere and have something to eat. Better put some clothes on—my mind is working overtime trying to figure out what you've got on underneath that robe."

The low pitched intimacy of his words worked their sensual magic on Nicole. Firmly intrigued by this man who was like no other she had ever met, she turned and walked into the privacy of her bedroom. Stripping off the robe with shaky hands, she let it drop to the floor. Her pulse raced wildly and her heart was skipping beats all over the place. She dressed mechanically, hardly realizing what she was doing, but her ears were finely tuned to his movements. He called out to her from the lounge.

"By the way, how's Richard?"

"He's out of town. As you probably know," she called back.

"What makes you think I would know anything about Richard?"

"You're a detective, remember?" she mocked, throwing his own words back at him. She heard him laugh softly. The sound came from menacingly close by, as if he had gravitated toward the hall that led into her bedroom. She finished dressing quickly with one eye on the door, never sure what he might do next.

When she finally emerged he was standing in the shadows of the hallway waiting, just as she had expected, lounging against the wall, the granite sensuality in full play. She marveled silently at the seemingly inexhaustible confidence and sheer nerve that abounded inside him. Where other men would spend time and energy wooing a woman, Jake just walked in and took what he wanted, whenever he wanted. Women probably dropped whatever they were doing to accommodate him. She was in danger of doing that herself.

The steely glint of his eyes never left hers as his long tanned fingers slipped inside his pocket for a cigarette. Beneath the deceptively casual stance, there was that ever present alien element, something coiled inside him that she couldn't put a name to. Once again she tried to pinpoint exactly what it was, but eventually gave up. Because she didn't have the answers.

They walked out into the living room and surveyed each other in silence. She took a good look at him for the first time since he had arrived. Dressed casually in a black polo-style knit shirt that spanned the impressive width of his shoulders, he was formidable. For a moment she was mesmerized by the fine, sun-bleached hair on his forearms, the sinful biceps flexing as he lit the cigarette.

"Ready?" he inquired. His gaze slid over her, not bothering to disguise his male interest in her feminine allure. The strong, mutual physical attraction jumped between them like a living flame.

They walked into a steak house that had once been a hostelry. Beveled mirrors gleamed like satin on the walls, which were covered by hundreds of black-and-white photographic studies. Deeply buttoned leather booths and the dramatic black-and-white-mosaic floor gave the steak house an early-twentieth-century look. A harried-looking waiter wearing a black bow tie, white shirt and long white apron led them to a table. Jake's proprietorial hand rested on the curve of Nicole's waist as they made their way among the tables in the small, crowded restaurant. The sound of subdued voices and clinking cutlery surrounded them.

When they were seated in a booth with menus in front of them, Nicole felt like some player watching herself from the wings of a stage, caught up in a drama for which she had never auditioned.

"I can't believe I'm actually sitting here with you."
She tossed her hair away from her high cheekbones
and the silver hoops in her ears with the tiny dangling
seahorses clinked musically. She was unable to understand the dragnet of her own emotions. The animal
brilliance in the gray eyes across the table told her Jake
had no such problems.

"I wanted you to get to know the man behind the
badge. I told you that in the club."

"Is that possible?" The silent look in her eyes rejected the suggestion. "Malcolm implied that it wasn't
easy to get to know you, that you were a loner and that
danger meant nothing to you."

"I'm no different than any other guy and no more
difficult to get to know." An approaching waiter distracted him. They gave their orders and as soon as the
man was out of earshot, Jake picked up the thread of
their conversation.

"What do you want to know about me?"

Nicole linked her fingers in front of her, studying
them, trying to extricate herself from the power of his
intimidating aura. "Do you realize how ludicrous that
question sounds to me after what happened in that
dark corner last night? You had your hands all over
me and I don't even know if you're married. For all I
know you could have a wife and six children tucked
away somewhere."

"Relax I'm not married. I've never been married,"
he said dismissively. "I was born and raised in Florida not far from here. My father is in real estate. He's
very successful at it. My mother died years ago. After
college I joined the police force. I've been with the
Miami Police Department for more than ten years."

He paused, leaning back in the seat. "Anything else you want to know?"

"Any distinguishing marks?" Her tone scoffed at the bare boned account.

He teased her openly with dangerous macho charm. "I'll show you all of them when you get to know me better. Every last one." She barely managed to keep a straight face.

"You know something," she said speculatively. "Maybe I would have found out more about you by pulling your personnel file. Is that all there is? Just the cold bare facts? Where you were born, where you went to school et cetera? Haven't you ever been in love? Weren't you ever engaged?"

"I was engaged once. But we broke it off by mutual agreement." His fingers tapped a knife idly as he studied it.

"That's surprising. You being so flexible and easygoing and all," she taunted softly.

His gaze shot to her face with a silent warning. "I'm easygoing when you get to know me. You'd be surprised just how easygoing I can be."

The waiter returned, serving them with steaming platters and a carafe of wine. When the waiter retreated she watched Jake heap mushrooms on top of a thick juicy steak, then dump copious amounts of Worcestershire sauce over it all.

"All right. It's your turn, Nicole."

"What do you mean?"

"I want to hear about you."

Since he had told her practically nothing about himself, she didn't feel like giving away too much, either. She leaned back and sipped her wine, studying him for a moment over the rim of the glass. Then she taunted him with some of his own observations about her.

"You acted like you knew so much about me last night. You told me how I've been lying to myself. You pointed out what I'm afraid of. You finished by telling me what I really want—namely you. I'm surprised that you even ask."

A faint smile touched his mouth. "Last night in the club I was playing on some strong hunches, going on blind instincts because you wouldn't let me near you. I wasn't too far off base, was I?" His steady gaze challenged her. "They got results," he added.

Her face warmed at the memory. She couldn't refute that.

"But that's not what I'm after," he continued. "If you won't volunteer any information, let me ask you a question. Why does my being a cop make you so uptight?" He leaned forward hunching his shoulders. His gray eyes pierced hers.

"Maybe I don't know you well enough to answer that."

The quick hard dangerous charm flashed at her again. "Come on, Nicole. We covered a lot of ground in that dark corner."

Her skin felt hot now. The knowledge that he was right surfaced in her eyes. A handful of hours. She had known him only a handful of hours and yet she felt that he had already carved out a place in her life for himself.

"Your father's a cop," he prompted. "You should have seen the good as well as the negative side."

"When I was growing up all I saw was what his being a cop did to my parents' marriage, and especially what it did to my mother. Officially she died from an embolism, but I never believed that. When my mother died, I connected the two—the strained marriage and her death. The two have been connected in my mind ever since I was a child. I find them difficult to separate even now. I never want to end up like her and I'm not going to put myself in that position ever."

He looked at her for a moment, absorbing that information. "Maybe it wasn't the job that was the real reason for the trouble at home. Did you ever think of that?"

"What do you mean?"

"I mean it could have been a lot of things. Who knows what goes on between a man and his wife, that special chemistry that other people don't feel? I doubt it was any one thing. It could have been lots of things you were too young to understand. Suppose there was another woman? How old were you at the time when all this was going on?"

"Nine or ten. But there was never another woman. I would have known or heard something, picked up on it somehow. My parents weren't like that." She laughed scornfully, dismissing the remark out of hand.

Cool, calculating gray eyes measured her response. "You're still looking at your parents the way a child sees them. Your father's a man, isn't he? Why was it so impossible?"

She frowned, perplexed because it had never occurred to her to even ask such a question. She had to search her mind for a more plausible reason than just her belief that it would never have happened.

"I would have heard. There was never a whisper of anything like that."

"Maybe you're right." He let her comments go, turning his attention to another tack. "What about my hunches about you and Richard?" He grinned and the quick, hard, dangerous charm was back.

"You were right about Richard, at least in some respects. I do think life with Richard would be very...quiet." His eyes drilled into hers with cynical amusement. She was hiding from the truth again. "All right...dull," she conceded. "Maybe there is some vital spark missing."

"Now you're making sense."

He smiled and hailed the waiter to bring them some rolls. Nicole sat twirling the stem of the wineglass between her fingers. His hand clamped down on hers. For a moment he studied her with a mixture of emotions in his eyes, as if he couldn't make up his mind about something. Nicole was beginning to formulate some very strong impressions about this brawny, sensual pirate herself. It prompted her to tell him what she thought about him. She tilted her head to one side playfully.

"Would you like me to tell you what makes you tick?"

"Do you think you can?" he challenged, laughing at the suggestion.

"I think I can make a stab at it. I would start by saying you're very dedicated to your job. There are no personal attachments that I can see. But that doesn't mean there aren't any women. Women are—entertainment. I don't think you have ever had a serious relationship with a single one, not even the woman you were engaged to."

"What makes you think that? Besides the fact that I was never married?"

"Because you don't care what kind of impression you're making. You've got colossal nerve because you're completely uninhibited by feelings of any kind except the ones below your belt."

"Take it from me, that's what drives most men." He grinned.

"Maybe, but most men wonder or worry about what kind of impression they're making, at least in some respects. Some of them worry about being rejected. Others worry about saying or doing something that might turn a woman off. And some worry about revealing something about themselves that a woman might use intentionally or unintentionally. But none of those things applies to you because you don't give a damn about anything. You probably make your move, take what you want and walk away without thinking twice."

He leaned forward, the hunched line of his shoulders making him look bigger and more predatory than usual—and completely unrepentant. "Suppose you're right. What do you think I should do? Get all choked up about it?"

"I don't think so. It gets results, as you just pointed out," she mocked him back. "It enables you to do and get exactly what you want without involving any of your feelings."

"Is that all you've figured out?" His narrowed eyes and the impassive expression on his face told her that he wasn't completely unaffected by her words.

"Not quite," she said, warming to the subject. "I also doubt whether you've ever sincerely apologized to any woman for anything. Tonight, when you came to the door with that phony apology about being out of line, was a prime example. You didn't really expect me to believe that did you?"

"So you don't think I was being sincere?" His cold smile confirmed it.

"I'd stake my life on it. I'd stake my life on something else, too."

"What's that?"

"I'll bet that you've never once said 'I love you' to any of the women you've known."

"Maybe I never felt like saying it." Their eyes locked for a long moment before he continued. "But there's one thing you haven't figured out yet, hotshot. You haven't figured out what happened in that dark corner. Or why it happened."

"I wouldn't attach too much importance to what happens in dark corners. We all behave recklessly from time to time," she shot back.

He grinned again with maddening ease. "I never attach too much importance to what happens in dark corners, either. But I know when something happens. I know when I've got more than a foot in the door. Now why don't we stop sniping at each other. It's time we started to enjoy ourselves together."

He was totally relaxed and in control. He monitored the look in her eyes with a lazy flash of sensual amusement and to her own amazement she did start to enjoy herself. The tension drained away and they sat talking easily over coffee and dessert. The invisible barriers lowered temporarily between them. They talked about their jobs, about Miami and the people they came into contact with. She liked listening to him. He had an easy relaxed way of talking, a ready wit and a keen observant intelligence that didn't miss much. Thoroughly bemused and beguiled, she watched the changing expressions in his eyes, then stole a glance across the hard cheekbones down to the tapered angle of his jaw. But while she was studying his handsome face with fascination, he, too, seemed to be absorbing everything about her. When he looked at his watch and announced there was a film playing at a nearby theater and asked her if she would like to see it, to her continuing surprise it seemed the most natural thing in the world to say yes.

He paid the bill and they rose from the table. She stood beside him trying to shake off the powerful effect he had on her. But at the same time, she found she didn't want it to end. It was a familiar feeling by now.

Inside the darkened theater he sprawled his leanly muscled frame in the seat next to hers. He caught her hand. With their fingers laced and his thigh grazing hers, they both had trouble concentrating on the film.

On the way home from the theater Jake asked if she'd like to take a walk on the beach. After sitting through a meal and a film, Nicole found the idea of a walk on the beach an appealing one. They started down the beach listening to the hypnotic pull and suck of the waves on the moon silvered sand. Bending over, she pulled off her sandals. He paused watching her.

"I love to walk barefoot in the sand," she said, holding her shoes in one hand as they resumed walking.

Thoughts of Jake and her father kept running through Nicole's mind. The quiet peace of the night, the easy rapport they had shared toward the end of the meal made her bold. Staring down at her feet sinking into the soft sand she took the plunge. "What happened between you and my father? When I told my father I met you, well, to be perfectly honest he wasn't happy about it. He doesn't like you for some reason. What happened between you two to cause all the bad feeling?"

Her questions hung in the night air. Jake halted and turned to look at her. His reaction was so intimidating she wished she could drag the question back. While her pulse rocketed, the sound of the pounding surf in the distance was the only sound between them.

A faint ironic smile touched his lips. "Why don't you ask him, Nicole?"

"I have. But it was like coming up against a brick wall. I couldn't get anywhere."

"What did he say?"

"He has very strong opinions. He doesn't want me to see you. But he has never given me any clear reasons why. He said that he didn't like you, but he wouldn't tell me why. He also said that you were too smart for your own good, but he didn't enlarge on that, either." Her gaze slid sideways to measure the effect of her words. Cynicism flickered across the hardening features of his face.

"Let's get something straight. I don't give a damn what your father does or doesn't think about me. There's no love lost between us. In fact, we hate each other's guts." A sardonic flash of amusement accompanied his words.

"Well, aren't you going to tell me why?"

"I've got nothing to say."

"It would be easier to understand if I knew something about it. I would know better how to deal with the situation." The thought occurred to her that if they kept on seeing each other, an explanation of some kind might help smooth over the awkwardness.

"You want to find out? You find out from him." Jake's attitude was just as irritating and mystifying as her father's.

"I don't see why you can't tell me." She dug in her heels.

"You don't have to know. It doesn't matter."

"It does matter. Why won't you tell me?"

"No, it doesn't matter." Irritation and impatience threaded through his tone. For a moment, she just stood, confused and staring at him, then her own temper unraveled. She didn't want to be fobbed off with "it doesn't matter" or "I don't care."

The simmering silence lengthened between them until Jake ended it. "You want to know what matters, Nicole? I'll show you what matters."

Everything inside her tensed at the look in his eyes. Before she could move Jake gripped her arms and dragged her up against his hard body. Her hands pushed forcefully, but his embrace was almost cruel in its demand for gratification. He held her prisoner.

"This is all that matters between us, Nicole." He breathed the words low and taut against her lips. Hard and hungry, his mouth captured hers, mingling desire with something nameless. His assault on her senses was all consuming. The wild passion she felt for the man holding her locked in his arms surged out of nowhere. Trembling with need, she clasped her hands around his neck. His hard-edged sensuality dragged the response he wanted from her. Everything faded but their mutual desire and exploration of each other. She pressed into him, her body sending out heady messages. His lips trailed a slow, fevered path along her face, to her neck, then back to her mouth where he renewed his teasing expertise. A deep yearning was born between them that developed rapidly as they swayed and moved in the intoxicating silent ritual of love, timeless but unique to each individual. As their mounting desire escalated, Jake demanded more to feed its heady glow. His hands released the buttons of her knit top. He pushed it off her bare shoulder, and slipped his hand inside, closing over the swell of her breast. With a rough sound of pleasure in his throat, he bit the side of her neck as if he wanted to devour her whole.

The fire blazed hotter. They maneuvered and jockeyed into closer positions, unable to find that ultimately satisfying position they both craved. Her fingers dug into his neck and shoulders for support as the ground seemed to open up beneath her feet. Drunk with her own awakening desire, she moved her hips in an unconscious invitation. His hands clamped down on them, locking her intimately against him. Their kisses deepened, growing rougher with an insatiable urgency. With his free hand, Jake bunched her skirt up around her hips. His breathing thickened in her ear and his movements became almost compulsive. Burying his face into the curve of her neck, he clasped her hip into his hardening body. A thick sensuality simmered between them like heat rising off a tarmac road, contrasting with cool damp and sand squeezed between her toes as she strained into him. Turning his head to the side for a restless movement, she sensed him fighting for control, sensed him trying to still the chiming needs of his body. Desire clawed at her like a living thing; it attacked her arms, making them heavy, it attacked her knees, threatening to buckle them out from under her. For a fleeting moment she wanted only to lie down on the cool damp sand.

But Jake obviously had a better place in mind. He fought for the control that never quite eluded him, while his rugged body shuddered with the effort it was costing him. His voice thick and low, he said. "Let's go somewhere."

But his words gave Nicole time to think, blowing the haze of desire from her mind.

Tightening his hands on her waist, he repeated his demand, "I said, let's go somewhere. My place."

"No," she snapped, pushing out of his arms. Her common sense was returning with a vengeance. Suddenly they were both struggling for some kind of control over the situation. It was a contest to see who was going to get the upper hand. For a long moment they stood looking at each other. Then taking a shaky step backward, she bent to pick up the sandals she'd dropped in the heat of the moment. She brushed the sand from her feet and slipped on the sandals.

"I've got to be getting back," she announced quietly, not looking at him. "It must be getting late."

He didn't bother to disguise the frustration in his tone. He jeered at her while she smoothed down her skirt and rebuttoned her loosened top. "Are you going to pretend that what just happened didn't happen, Nicole?''

She straightened and gazed steadily at him. "No. I'm not going to pretend it didn't happen. I'm not going to pretend anymore that you don't get to me." In the dark she could just make out the rough outline of his face and the silvery glitter of his eyes. "What I don't understand is *why* it's happening. Neither of us wants it to happen."

"Desire is a funny thing. Sometimes there's no explaining it." The cynicism in his eyes ate into her. It cooled whatever ardor was left.

"I guess you'd better take me home now."

"If that's the way you want it," he conceded easily enough, but she could see he didn't like it. He was obviously experienced enough to know when to push and when to ease off.

They walked back to the car, both of them lost in their own thoughts, not wanting to say anything that would give away what they were thinking. Nicole felt a little breathless as if she had been running too fast. Drugged by desire, her common sense was desperately trying to come through. The tall, enigmatic man walking beside her wielded a lethal combination—a potent masculinity mixed with the force and intelligence to know exactly what he wanted and exactly how to get it.

When they reached her home, he turned to her in the shadows of the car. "I want to see you again."

"Call me."

His eyes searched her face. That was all she would commit herself to at the moment, until she had time to think, until she came down from this high-flying emotional plane his presence induced. He got out of the car and walked around to her side and pulled open the door. When she got out, he leaned over and delivered a hard possessive kiss, pressing her back against the side of the car.

When Jake left Nicole he drove back to the beach. He liked the solitary atmosphere of the beach at night when he wanted to think. Slamming the car door behind him, he paused to light a cigarette. Hunching his shoulders, he cupped the flame against the night breeze, then leaned back against the car. He watched the glowing ember between his fingers burn as Nicole's words about him at dinner echoed inside his head. Things weren't going quite the way he had anticipated.

He could feel himself getting involved with her more than he wanted to. The sexual attraction had an emotional side that already showed signs of deepening. He swore silently at himself. He was starting to think too much. He didn't like that. He was starting to ask himself questions. He didn't like that, either. The possibility that Nicole was a woman he could fall in love with rose up in front of his eyes. He acknowledged it, but the lust for revenge still ran like a deep dark current, mastering the other newer feeling. He knew something else he didn't like much. They were headed for an explosive situation. He could see it coming as clearly as he could see the glowing tip of the cigarette in front of his eyes. He wasn't sure what would happen, but if love complicated the physical attraction between them, there was going to be a heavy price to pay. But he couldn't stop things now.

He knew his nature by now; when he wanted something badly he pulled out all the stops to go after it. He had made up his mind that he wanted Nicole Bradley *and* revenge. He just couldn't seem to separate one from the other.

Chapter 5

"Was everything all right? Did you enjoy the meal?" the deferential waiter inquired.

"It was delicious," Nicole murmured, smiling warmly at him.

Richard's voice echoed hers. "Absolutely delicious. Will you bring us coffee, please?" The waiter bowed, cleared the rest of the dishes, then carried away the silver tray balanced on his shoulder.

Nicole's gaze swept the room. They were dining out at one of those glittering Miami Beach hotels that boasted a floor show, dinner and dancing. People were rising from tables to dance to the infectious beat of the Latin American band.

"Let's dance." Standing, Richard reached out a hand. Looking up at him, she slipped her hand into his and followed his lead. On the dance floor he studied her with warmth in his dark eyes.

"What did you do while I was away?" he asked, and her conscience pricked her. A blank expression slid into her eyes as she covered up the tumult of emotions his question triggered.

"Oh, nothing much."

His gaze slid to the black dress with narrow straps that plunged almost as low in front as it did in the back. "I like the dress."

"Do you? I'm glad."

She smiled at him, knowing she was dressed provocatively, and that her behavior was following suit. It didn't tax her brain too much to figure out why. A sense of quiet desperation lingered inside her. She could pinpoint the exact time and place that had spawned it—the evening out with quick, hard and dangerous Jake Slater. She couldn't get that night out of her mind, but she had to. That walk on the beach, and those moments in his arms were conspiring against her. Nicole was desperately trying to hang on to what she stubbornly told herself she wanted. Executing a complete about-face after their evening out together, Nicole had refused all Jake's calls. Struggling for some semblance of normalcy, she wanted to come down off the high-flying plane of turbulent emotions induced by Jake's invasion into her life. Her aversion to cops had reasserted itself with a vengeance. Now she struggled to remember her father's warnings instead of how it felt to be drugged with desire in Jake's arms.

And as soon as Richard got back into town, he had called to make a date. What was she going to do? Should she tell him that she had met a sensual pirate who was stealing her out from underneath his nose, bit by bit? Should she tell him that she was teetering on a knife edge of self-control. For God's sake, stay calm, she warned herself. You don't have to tell him anything. Because nothing is going to happen. You're not going to *let* anything happen.

"I dislike it when I have to go out of town. I miss you." Richard's soft words whispered across the shell of her ear. He was so attentive, so true, that her guilty conscience clawed at her.

"I don't like it much, either." Soft affection filled her eyes when she gazed into his dark searching ones. The sincerity in her tone was unmistakable. But she couldn't tell him the reason why.

When Richard was around she didn't feel so vulnerable, so exposed to Jake's lethal brand of attraction. While dancing in Richard's arms on the crowded floor, she felt a strong surge of conflicting emotions, forcing her to make comparisons between Richard and Jake—comparisons that weren't fair to Richard.

For the rest of the evening Nicole maintained the illusion that she was having a fantastic time. She felt like some kind of consummate actress. When she and Richard reached the seclusion of his car in the parking lot, he pulled her into his arms, his kisses more ardent than usual. Nicole knew that it was because she was encouraging him, but she couldn't seem to stop herself. Nor did she want to admit to herself why. Richard's face hovered inches away in the dark. His hand pushed aside the narrow strap from her shoulder, which he softly kissed.

"Come to my place—stay with me tonight. I know we said we would wait, but I'm only human, Nicole. God, it's been so long and I'm no saint. Can't we go back to my place?"

The battle was raging inside her between the man who held her in his arms, and the interloper in her mind. "All right," she breathed against his lips. Something inside her retaliated. It wasn't fair that a pair of silvered eyes could rule her heart with one long look. It wasn't fair that they could steal her heart without her permission.

They drove to Richard's condo through darkened palm-tree-lined boulevards, and once they were inside, Richard kissed her again. His kisses were warm and pleasant; it didn't matter that there was no mad rush of desire, none of the fiery urgency that she experienced with Jake. A burning love that left nothing but a trail of pale ashes when it was over was no love at all. That was what loving Jake would mean. She was opting for the sure thing. Loving Richard made much more sense. Love was supposed to make sense, wasn't it? Nicole was still rationalizing, still trying to convince herself when Richard's voice momentarily stopped her.

"Do you want a drink or anything?"

"I don't think so." Shaking her head slowly, she smiled encouragingly at him. When he moved closer, Jake's image flashed into her mind. She struggled to blot him from her mind.

Richard lowered his head to the line of her soft mouth.

"I don't want anything, either," he murmured huskily with his lips close to hers. "All I want is you."

Standing motionless, she tilted back her head to receive his kiss. He whispered her name softly over and over again. All Nicole could hear were Jake's deep resonant tones, echoing inside her head. She closed her

eyes when Richard started covering her face and neck
with light soft kisses. A sense of detachment was
stealing over her. The searing sound of her zipper being lowered filled the air. Then his hands pushed the
straps down off her shoulders. When she opened her
eyes, Richard's flushed face reflected his mounting
excitement, but he left her feeling cold. She watched
him pull back to loosen his tie and strip it off along
with his jacket. Inside she was dying slowly, inch by
inch, as each garment hit the floor. All the time, Jake,
with his leering granite sensuality, leaned indolently in
a corner of her mind, watching with cynical amusement. *How long are you going to go on lying to yourself, Nicole?*

Richard moved closer again and whispered her
name as he unhooked her lacy bra with deft fingers.
With a sense of defiance she returned his kisses, resting her hands on his shoulders. He murmured her
name over and over again. He was so sweet, so con-
siderate, but she just didn't love him.

Suddenly, she clenched her eyes in anguish. Jake
had won. What was she doing just going through the
motions? Why? To prove something that wasn't true?
Without warning, Nicole twisted violently away, pulling the narrow straps up her arms.

Richard's soft voice exploded behind her. "Nicole,
what's the matter?" The fierce tones forced her to turn
around to confront him, her eyes filled with remorse.

Nearly choking on the words, she said, "Nothing.
I'm sorry. I can't go through with this. I just can't."

Half-undressed, he stared at her with a glazed look.
Confusion and disbelief mingled in his dark eyes as he
reached out and caught her shoulders, dragging her

forward. Nicole's hand clutched the unzipped dress to her breast. She couldn't go to bed with him just because she felt sorry for him or because it was the kind and fair thing to do. Or because he had been patient and waited a long time. She couldn't leave passion behind, leaving out all those naked vulnerable inexplicable feelings that went with it. Those deepest expressions of desire didn't exist for her and Richard. Even if what she felt for Jake didn't make much sense, she knew now she wouldn't settle for anything less, for some anemic version of the same thing with Richard.

"I can't sleep with you because I don't love you."

With a hurt look in his eyes he accused her softly. "What are you trying to do to me? Nicole, what are you trying to do to us?"

"I'm sorry. I should never have encouraged you. This is all my fault." Finding it difficult to look him in the eye, she continued. "I don't think we should see each other anymore. Honestly, I don't know what I'm doing half the time these days."

"What brought this on?" She had rarely seen Richard lose his composure, but it eluded him now and she certainly couldn't blame him. He grabbed hold of her again. "I feel like a prize fool.... I thought the whole evening was going fantastically well. You let me take you here, then you spring this on me. Now you tell me that you don't know whether you're coming or going. Well, that makes two of us."

"I'd better leave," she murmured with a contrite look. "Don't bother to take me home. I'll call myself a cab. We'll talk some other time. I can't explain everything now."

"You've got to make up your mind, Nicole. This ambivalence, this not knowing, just isn't good enough. It's dangerous. People go around doing all kinds of crazy things when they're in two minds." Still staring at her fixedly, he jabbed a finger at her, adding ominously, "You know, I've seen people like you in court. You're beginning to remind me of one of my clients."

"Richard," she groaned. His words made her realize that she had to tell him about Jake. The truth had to come out whether it made sense or not. Turning around she confronted him. "There's something I should tell you."

"Now we're getting somewhere," he said with a derisive laugh.

"I went out with someone else while you were out of town."

For a moment he stood silent and motionless, then he spoke. "I thought we had an understanding. Why did you make a date with someone behind my back?"

"It just happened—I didn't plan on it. He turned up at the house and asked me to go out to dinner with him. And I went."

"Who is it?"

"Jake Slater—the homicide detective from Miami Police Department?"

"How do you feel about him?"

"I wish I knew the answer. The only honest answer I can give you is that I've never felt this way about anybody before. I'm sorry, Richard."

On Monday, Malcolm Rogers called her into his office.

"Do you want to take over the police beat?"

She looked at him in amazement. He was absolutely serious, she realized.

"John is leaving, as you know. I've been trying to get someone from another paper, but it fell through. Nobody else wants the police beat."

"Why do you think I want it?"

"You have an instinct for it, Nicole. Don't tell me you're not interested after writing that brilliant series on raised recruiting standards and declining incidents of corruption. I know you have a talent in this direction, Nicole. Call it a special affinity because of your background. Help us out until I can lure a reporter from another paper." She made no reply and Malcolm saw the indecision in her face. "At least think it over, Nicole."

She rose from her chair and walked over to the window, thinking about what he was saying. It was true—she did have an inclination in that direction—anything to do with police work fascinated her. But her mind instantly focused on two things. The old emotional seesaw came into play. She wanted to get away from the world of cops. She wanted to get away from Jake. The job would just pull her back toward both. But the lure of covering the police beat was proving stronger than the negative factors. Besides, the police beat would keep her so busy that she wouldn't have time to think too much about Jake. The pace of work was almost manic, she had heard.

"All right, for a moment say that I agree with you. Maybe I do, because of my background, have a natural flair for this kind of work. But the hours and the work load don't appeal to me at all. How can I have any kind of social life with the police radio informing me there's been another homicide down in Little Havana?''

Malcolm as always was ready with an answer. "No one's asking you to do it forever. Why don't you think of it as something you're going to do for the time being, a stopgap measure."

She tossed the idea around in her head. The job *was* tempting. It was also a step up out of general reporting, she concluded. If she took it, Malcolm couldn't easily put her back into general reporting again. He would have to give her something else.

"I'll take it."

"John leaves on Friday."

On the first day of Nicole's new job she walked over to the city desk and looked disbelievingly at two homicide reports that had come in during the night. She was dismayed. There were already two and the day had only just begun.

"Malcolm, I can't possibly cover everything that comes across this desk. How many stories do you want me to write?"

"Pick out the juiciest ones." Her mouth curved into a wry smile as she wondered what the criteria were for those choices.

When she reached the site of the first homicide on her list, she walked inside a luxurious condominium tower and took the elevator up to the fifth floor. Stepping out of the elevator she could hear the bustle of police personnel and two-way radios echoing down the thickly carpeted hallway. Her mind focused on the job at hand, which was to gather information and put together a puzzle about a person now deceased. She knew that cops were naturally wary of the press, and she wasn't sure how much information she would be able to get from them. Malcolm said she would have to rely heavily on witnesses and other sources to put together a good story.

She followed the sounds to an open door. Inside, half a dozen people were busy at the crime scene. One corner of the living room was cordoned off by yellow ropes. A corpse lay facedown in a pool of blood. Out of the corner of her eye she watched the detectives and a uniformed policeman carry on a conversation with their backs to her. No one was paying much attention to her. With people milling around it was difficult to see anything so she stepped nearer to the cordoned-off area and peered cautiously over the ropes, trying to get a closer look at the body. With the head twisted to one side she could see the corpse was male, Hispanic and in his middle thirties.

A low-pitched voice shot out of nowhere.

"Hey you! Do you want to get yourself arrested and thrown in jail?"

Startled, Nicole turned around quickly, almost losing her balance and stumbling back over the ropes. Two detectives loomed up in front of her. The blazing sheen of one detective's eyes made the other fade into nothingness. Her heart developed an erratic pattern of beats as Jake's eyes drilled silently into her. He was pure macho cop. She had wandered onto his turf. The look in his eyes said he wasn't going to let her forget it for one single minute.

"What are *you* doing here?" Jake's question bristled with innuendo. Foremost was the implication challenging her right to be there at all.

With slowly maddening defiance she reached into her pocket and held up her press card in front of his nose. He silently acknowledged it, but there was no outward sign, not even a glimmer of recognition that he knew her. Apparently satisfied that she had a right to be there, he said, "The scene of a crime cannot be tampered with. You don't go too near it. You don't step on it. You don't touch anything. You don't even breathe too hard near it. Do I make myself clear?"

"Perfectly." Her eyes flashed a subtle warning at him that had no effect whatsoever.

"Why are you here instead of John?"

"John has left for good. I'm covering the police beat now." Undercurrents kept shooting back and forth between them.

Suddenly a voice called out from the doorway, taking his attention away from Nicole temporarily. "Hey, Emilio, forensic is here." Jake's neatly cropped head turned to watch his partner go. When Emilio was out of earshot, he turned back to face her. Only then did he act as if he knew her. "Did Malcolm talk you into this or did you volunteer?"

"Malcolm was the one who suggested it. I took him up on the offer because I wanted to get out of general reporting."

"Is that the only reason?" The steel glitter of his eyes focused on her face. "I always knew you'd end up in my world. You're full of contradictions, Nicole. You can't stay away from it, can you? I thought you didn't like cops."

"It's the work that fascinates me, not the men who do it," she pointed out with a little defiant smile.

"Is that so. Well, I remember you acting pretty interested on one or two occasions." His meaning was unmistakable. Her face warmed at the recollection of just how interested she had acted.

"I didn't take the job to run into you, if that's what you're thinking."

"Do you really want me to tell you what I'm thinking?"

Jake's nearness was having all the usual effects—her pulse rate rocketed and she had difficulty concentrating on what she was doing or saying. Forcing herself to focus on her job, she got out her notebook.

"Can you fill me in on some of the details, Detective Slater? If it's not too much trouble."

"There will be an official police statement printed. Why don't you try reading it?" His clipped response made her blood surge. Lifting her gaze from the notebook, she searched his eyes. Was he going to make life as difficult as he could for her because she'd turned him down? It looked that way.

"Sorry, that won't do. I can't write a good story on those miserable two- and three-line statements the department issues. I want to know some of the details surrounding the case."

"What do you want to know, hotshot?" Where before it was *Sunshine* and *honey,* now it was *hotshot,* she fumed silently.

"The name is Nicole Bradley," she reminded him.

"It must have slipped my mind. But there are a lot of things that haven't slipped my mind."

"Stop it," she hissed. Then she looked uneasily around to see if anyone was watching. No one was. Pointing to the corpse on the floor, she tried to get on with her job. "Who is he?"

"Roberto Ramirez." She kept her eyes on her notepad; it was safer not to look at him. But she felt his eyes boring into her.

"Is this drug related?"

"We think so."

She shifted uneasily while he hovered over her with an air of possession. Hot blood flushed her cheekbones under his proprietorial stare. She forced herself to concentrate on her job. "What part of the business was he involved in?"

"Money laundering. He must have been holding out on somebody, holding back a percentage for himself. He just came back from a business trip in the Cayman Islands. We have a few good leads but we have to check them out. That's all I can tell you."

"Any witnesses?"

"Several people heard the shots. As usual, no one saw anything. His girlfriend over there says they had been out all night at a club, then had gone for an early-morning swim on the beach. She was in the bathroom showering when she heard the shots. When she came out she found him like that. He was shot through the back of the head, as you can see. It looks like a professional did the job."

"Does he have a record?"

"A mile long. Check the police files, hotshot."

Not making the mistake of rising to the bait she appealed to his professionalism. "Detective Slater, we both have a job to do. I hope personal feelings aren't going to enter into this.''

A long staring silence passed between them. Jake spoke volumes with his silences. He used them the way other men used words. The raw ache of longing stirred deep inside her. Seeing him again was proving much harder than she had thought.

''You're crazy if you think I can treat you like just another reporter from the press. I've got one more thing to say to you.''

''I'm afraid to ask. What is it?'' she retorted flippantly, trying to offset the effect of his words.

''Where do you think you're going dressed like that?''

''What do you mean?''

''If you're going to play at being a reporter on the police beat, you're not dressed for it, honey.''

Her temper flared at his persistent needling. ''I'm not *playing* at anything. I don't play around at things. I'm going to do the job to the best of my ability.''

His gaze trailed pointedly over the outfit, outlining her soft curves down to the heels on her shoes. ''Homicides happen in all kinds of places. In deserted isolated spots like swamps and fields. You may have to tramp through mud or wade through water or climb up onto a roof. I thought a cop's daughter would realize that.''

Embarrassed warmth suffused her skin. Not only because he was right, but because his blatant male look was stripping away what she wore. Her composure went with it.

His eyes narrowed—he wasn't through. "Speaking of playing around...how's Richard? If that's not playing around, what the hell is it?" he taunted softly.

The implication that she was wasting her time with Richard was all too clear. But the remark didn't deserve a response. In the blistering silence that followed she turned around and walked away.

She sensed him turning away, too, ignoring her as if she weren't there anymore, coolly shutting her out of his mind. She heard him talking to the forensic expert in low even tones. Her senses were reeling from seeing him again. He had been out to inflict damage and he had succeeded. Jake wasn't a man to turn the other cheek in any situation, especially when a woman had spurned him. She couldn't deny the impact his presence had on her.

Finally, her professionalism reasserted itself and she spent the next hour interviewing the woman in the corner and talking to various people in the condominium complex. She was correcting her notes as she walked out of the building and back to her car.

Jake's gaze followed her slowly when he thought no one was looking. Ostensibly he had stepped out onto the condo's balcony for a cigarette. Instead he stood watching Nicole exit the building and walk slowly toward her car. There was an inherent grace to her, a beauty that never failed to elicit a response from him. But she had turned away from him. After that night on the beach, the complete cutoff had surprised him. If it had been any other woman he wouldn't have given it another thought, but this one was definitely different. She had gotten to him and he didn't like it now any more than when he had first acknowledged that possibility. Only now there was a difference. He had this burning need to dominate her, to pay her back in kind for the way she had subtly dominated his thoughts since that night. It made him burn inside with a nameless anger that was almost equal in importance to the desire to get revenge on her father.

By the end of the day Nicole had covered three homicides, nothing unusual for Miami. She walked over to the city desk and talked with Malcolm. Then she went back to write up the "juiciest" one, using as much detail as possible, checking out more leads by telephone, trying to make the story come alive. She got home late that evening. After a light supper and a shower, she fell into bed exhausted. When she closed her eyes, Jake surged into her thoughts. Soon her mind was again hurtling like a freight train down that long dark forbidden tunnel where she knew she shouldn't go.

The days and weeks that followed were hectic and exciting. She covered all kinds of stories from missing persons to crimes of passion. From explosions of temper resulting in domestic violence to drug deals gone wrong. She saw the full panoply of the darker side of human nature. During all this time she tried unsuccessfully to blot Jake from her mind by losing herself in her work. But she ran into him again and again. Coiled, complex, professional and tough, he was completely unreadable. But more than once in unguarded moments she caught him looking at her. And on more occasions than she cared to admit he caught her doing the same thing. The expression in his eyes said the police beat was no place for a woman, making her wonder how he treated female cops. Or was it just one particular woman whom he didn't want to see on this beat? she wondered wryly. Sometimes, she couldn't help noticing his gaze sliding over her. Taking his advice, she dressed more casually, usually in a blazer, T-shirt and jeans, and she hardly cut a glamorous figure anymore. She flashed her press card in front of his nose whenever he called her Sunshine until he finally relented. But the look in his eyes said that he wasn't going to relent on some other things.

And now, on a Friday afternoon, she was walking away from covering a hit-and-run when Jake left his assistant and caught up with her. "How about some lunch?" he asked.

Laughing out loud, she started to turn but he caught her arm, pulling her back in one motion. She had attempted to walk away from him once too often. He wasn't letting her do it again.

"Isn't it time we both stopped kidding ourselves?"

The low-pitched words echoed in her ears as he looked at her. He appeared just as authoritative and arrogant and interested as ever. Nothing had changed. Her heart flipped over, paying no attention to her common sense. "I don't know what you mean."

"You know damned well what I mean. I want to talk to you. Let's go get ourselves some lunch."

Her empty stomach must have weakened her mind, because when he put his hand on her arm and spoke those same words again with a naked look of need in his eyes, she distinctly heard herself say yes. Surely one little lunch couldn't do any harm, she caught herself thinking.

When they reached a fast food restaurant, he propelled her toward one of the booths.

"Stay here. Don't run off. I'm going to buy you lunch. What do you want?"

"A hamburger and fries. But I'll pay for my own lunch, thanks." She reached into her shoulder bag with the hazy conviction that if she paid for her own meal she wouldn't come under his spell. But when the glint of his eyes locked with hers she knew she already had.

"Put your money away. When you're with me, I pay, Nicole." Her legs turned to rubber, and she sank into the booth with an air of surrender. After staring unseeingly into space until he returned with a tray, she watched him slide his leanly muscled, powerful frame into the seat opposite hers. Silently he handed over her hamburger and fries.

"You look tired. I'd like to get my hands on Malcolm for putting you on this. It's no place for a woman."

"I think I'm doing a good job. And I don't look tired," she protested, removing her large sunglasses. The thought occurred to her that they never agreed on anything.

Suddenly the police radio at his elbow went off. They heard the call voice identifying a 317—traffic accident with injuries. He ignored it.

"Mack will get that," he announced, taking a bite from his cheeseburger. He quickly washed it down with some coffee, like a man used to eating on the run. A slice of apple pie sat beside the coffee cup.

"I want to see you again," he said quietly between munches. His hand reached out and caught hers. His touch was electric. She didn't pull away. The look in her eyes told him he was going to get what he wanted. But it was more than her life was worth to give in easily.

"I told you how I feel about cops." She drew her hand away and bit into her hamburger. He stared at her in sizzling silence. If it were possible to swear silently with one's eyes, Jake did it then.

She gulped down what she had bitten off. "Who do you think killed Ramirez?" she asked, trying to stay on top of the situation. Then she bit into her hamburger again.

"Right now I don't give a bleep who killed Ramirez. I want to see you again." He stared at her with some kind of naked emotion in his eyes. Not sure what it was, she put down the hamburger, stunned. Where was that I-don't-give-a-damn attitude? Had she penetrated it somehow? Whatever it was she saw in his eyes touched her deeply. But a sense of self-preservation rallied to her defense.

"Look at us. Both of us sitting here waiting. Any minute now that radio is going to go off, dragging you away. Or I'm going to race off in the opposite direction. That's what it would be like if I let myself ... get involved with you. And that's only the half of it." The words *let myself love you* had almost slipped out.

"We already are involved." The short clipped response ricocheted back.

"It's doomed right from the start. This is an impossible relationship."

He shoved aside the remains of his hamburger. He looked uneasily around to make sure that no one was listening. "I've told myself that, too, but somehow it doesn't seem to matter. Now when am I going to see you?"

"I can't. I'm working late." Whatever came into her head, she said.

His hand caught hers again in a steellike grip, reminding her of his awesome strength. "Nicole, you're lying to me and to yourself."

"Does it matter?"

"It matters like hell," he exploded fiercely. The muscles in his jaw grew taut with the look of a man who had revealed more than he wished to. Then he relaxed. The look vanished and his face resumed its usual expression. His radio went off again; the dispatcher announced a 45. Lunch was swiftly coming to an end. Nicole could see that. She wondered idly what time he got home for dinner most evenings.

"Call me," she finally conceded against her better judgment.

"What's your number?" He tightened his grip, studying her through half-closed eyes like a man who expected another avenue of evasion. When she told him her unlisted number, he memorized it. Then his hand eased its pressure. She felt blood start to flow back through her fingers.

"You're wasting your time. I wouldn't call me if I were you."

"You're not me, Nicole. Remember that."

A squad car screeched to a halt outside for him. He gulped down the rest of his coffee and grabbed the wrapped apple pie from the tray, stuffing it into his pocket. They rose together and walked out into the blazing Florida sunshine.

She knew that when he called again she wouldn't have the willpower to say no. With a sense of resignation she slipped on her sunglasses. "Thanks for the lunch."

"My pleasure," he shot back, grinning at her with maddening ease.

The next morning Nicole's father's raised voice awakened her. She had been dreaming one of those wildly erotic dreams that one never wanted to wake up from. But even the marvelous dream couldn't blot out the strident tones of her father's voice as he told someone off on the telephone in the hallway. Her eyes widened instantly. All her instincts told her it was Jake. He'd said he would call. Her father slammed the phone down and strode out of the hallway.

She sat up slowly in bed. Her curling hair tumbled around her face and she ran her hands through it. Sliding the narrow straps of her nightgown back onto her shoulders, she pushed the covers aside, then stood up and pulled on a robe. Tying it tightly around her waist, she walked out into the living room. Her father stood there, his face black as thunder.

"Did I hear you shouting at someone on the phone?" she asked, still feeling half-asleep.

"You know who that was. It was that bastard Jake Slater." He muttered some explicit words underneath his breath. Her father always attempted to curb his more colorful language in front of his daughter. She tried to suppress a smile. The habit struck Nicole as comical even when he was obviously genuinely annoyed. She had been the apple of her father's eye for too long to be put off by his outbursts of temper. She faced him sleepily.

"If he calls here again, I'm going to have our phone number changed. How did he get the number anyway?"

"I gave it to him," she said quietly.

Her father turned on her with his eyes narrowed. "Has he called before when I wasn't here?"

"Yes. He has, but in person." Now she was the one who was getting annoyed. "Dad, you really shouldn't do things like that. It was my phone call. I can handle him."

Her father laughed scornfully. "You're wrong, Nicole. You can't handle him. No one can handle that guy. I know what he's after." Bemused, she stared at him. Her face flushed at her father's words. She averted her gaze, but she sensed her father's eyes still on her. They were both thinking the same thing.

"Maybe if you would explain to me why you feel this way about him I would pay more attention to what you're saying. As things stand I just think you're both too much alike, both too stubborn to smooth over your differences—whatever they are. You're both giving me a headache." She ran a distracted hand through her hair as she watched something flicker in the depths of her father's eyes. He looked like a man who was warring with something inside himself, as though he wanted to tell her something but couldn't bring himself to do it. There was a telltale sign of his frustration—the muscle in his jaw grew taut.

"Does Richard know that Jake's hanging around and calling you?"

"I told him about Jake last time I saw him." Clutching her robe in one hand, she was half listening for the telephone to ring again. At the same time, the question ran through her mind. How could one man cause so much trouble in so little time?

Her father's eyes mirrored his sense of disappointment at her reply. "I'm sorry to hear that, Nicole. I'm sorry to hear that you've ignored all my warnings. I don't know why you couldn't listen to me about Jake. God knows I don't tell you how to run your life."

She quirked a skeptical eyebrow at his remark.

"All right, maybe I do occasionally," he conceded. "I'm your father. What can you expect? You'll always be my daughter and I care what happens to you."

She looked up at him, with her heart in her eyes, appealing to him to understand. "I did try to stay away from him. But there's something about him...." She frowned and walked over to the patio doors, searching for the right words. "I can't seem to stop myself." There was complete and utter silence from the other side of the room. She couldn't see her father's face, but she knew her words had made a deep impression. When she swung around, her father's expression was tautly enigmatic.

"I am a grown woman, Dad. I have to decide for myself who I will see and who I won't see." Her words were quietly spoken. She was more than a little tired of her father's arrogance and high-handedness, even if it was well meant. More important, she found herself wanting to defend Jake. The tables were turning, the way they did in human relationships from time to time. Suddenly without warning, people found themselves on the opposite side from where they had been.

Warm relationships cooled, and old foes turned into friends, like foreign countries trying to strike some kind of peculiar balance. She and her father were now on opposing sides of some invisible fence.

Her father spoke quietly this time. If anything the effect was more powerful. "I'm going to ask you one more time as a personal favor to me. Promise me that you won't see him again, Nicole."

A sadness over having to go against him came into her heart. "I'm sorry, Dad. I can't promise that." It's gone too far for that now, she thought to herself. Her father looked suddenly defeated and weary. The look in his steel-blue eyes wrenched at her heart, but it didn't change her mind. Nicole knew that she and Jake had passed some invisible point. She wasn't turning away anymore. She walked into the kitchen. Her father strode out of the house, slamming the front door behind him. The sound made her flinch inwardly. It was a hard day for a father when he discovered that a man whom he despised ruled his daughter's heart.

Later that morning, after being unable to reach Nicole by phone, Jake came to the house. He beeped the horn of his car. When she walked outside he was leaning against the side of his car.

"I tried reaching you by phone this morning. Your father slammed the phone in my ear. Something tells me he hasn't changed his opinion about me." A smile tugged at the corners of his mouth. But cynicism shone in his eyes.

"Sometimes he loses his temper over nothing." Her expression and the tone of her voice were apologetic for her father's behavior. She was sure in her own mind that the enmity between her father and Jake stemmed from the fact that they were both very strong personalities and both unwilling to bend. It was probably over some petty disagreement or a case of them simply rubbing each other the wrong way.

"How about Richard? What would he say if he knew I was here?" He closed the distance between them and she invited him inside. When the door closed behind him, his hand reached to the curve of her waist, drawing her close.

"I've stopped seeing Richard," she admitted, feeling the pull of his eyes and watching his gaze slide down her face. His nearness and the touch of his hand were enough to arouse a heavy surge of desire. One look, one touch, was all it took.

"Why?" he queried softly.

"I realized that I wasn't in love with him, that I was never going to love him enough to marry him. As far as I'm concerned, it's over."

"Why was that? Did it have something to do with us?"

"Maybe," she admitted. His mouth curved slightly. He was satisfied with that much for now, his expression said.

"Why don't you get changed? We'll go someplace for lunch. Do you like lobster?"

"I love it."

"I know a place on the Intracoastal Waterway that serves great stuffed Florida lobster."

They smiled at each other. "I'll go in and get dressed. I won't be long."

When she emerged she was wearing a slim yellow dress that buttoned down the front, with a wide matching belt. Jake's lazy glance absorbed every detail. Her appearance was a far cry from the reporter covering the police beat he had seen on and off for the past few weeks. They walked out to his car and slid into opposite sides. The car hummed down the palm-tree-lined boulevards, with bougainvillea and hibiscus adding flashes of color.

"You know what puzzles me about you?" Jake wondered aloud.

"What?"

"Why is the hotshot reporter still living at home with her father?"

"Well, it's convenient, economic—"

He cut her short. "Don't give me that. That's not the real reason."

"I don't know," she retorted evasively. "I keep asking myself that same question. You were the one who said people didn't fall into neatly labeled categories, weren't you. All right. You tell me. Why am I still there?"

"Because cops and the whole life you *say* you hate is in your blood. You can't tear yourself away from it any more than I can. It's got a hold on you. That's why you're working the police beat. And that's one of the reasons why you can't ignore me."

She bristled, staring at him silently. Those were her very own thoughts. Coming from him, the truth was even less palatable than when she confronted it alone herself. What was she going to do about it? Was she going to spend the rest of her life seesawing back and forth between what she said she wanted and what she actually did want? A sense of hopeless frustration surged up inside her, along with a kind of anguished confusion. Didn't she know her own mind? Was she going to be one of those women who went through life never knowing what she wanted, never being happy?

"Well, am I right?"

"Maybe there's some truth to what you say." Her response was low-pitched and reluctantly made. With sharp perception her eyes narrowed on his rugged profile and angular jaw. "What about you?"

"What about me?" he countered. "Is there still more you want to know about me? Isn't your female curiosity satisfied yet?"

"There's plenty I would like to know but somehow I don't think you would tell me. I suspect I'm going to have to find out myself."

"You could be right," he announced in such a sober tone of voice that it made her uneasy. The expression on his face didn't change, but she sensed that she had disturbed one of those deep pools inside him that he kept hidden.

When he wasn't forthcoming, she probed some more. "Maybe there's one thing you could tell me."

"What's that?"

"Do you live with anyone?" She challenged him with her eyes, across the space of the bucket seats that separated them. With the top down on his car, the wind tossed her hair wildly around her face. Her hand caught it to shove it away.

With deep male amusement he laughed softly. "I live alone, hotshot, in a warehouse on the Miami River. That's where I'm taking you."

"What?" The blood surged inside her, like the wind rushing by the car.

He indicated his clothes—a black polo-style shirt and faded jeans. "I can't go dressed like this to the restaurant I'm taking you to. I have to wear a tie and jacket. Besides I want to show you where I live."

Her curiosity overshadowed any misgivings she might have had. When a woman caught herself falling in love with a man it was only natural to want to know everything about him.

"Feeling reckless today?" he taunted, with his eyes on the road, and a lazy, sensual smile deepening the corners of his mouth.

"I've always had a little wild streak in me, but until a certain macho cop stormed into my life I managed to keep it successfully contained."

"Maybe we should put it to the test."

"You bastard." Nicole laughed softly. "That's what you've been doing since the first minute we met."

"I'm glad we understand each other so well."

Chapter 6

"How does a policeman afford a Lotus Elan?" she asked when they stopped at a traffic light.

"My father has given me some very good advice and let me in on some lucrative property deals. I'm not on the take, if that's what you're wondering," he announced dryly.

"I never thought it for one minute," she murmured, laughing.

"Like hell you didn't," he shot back. Then his bold eyes grew serious. "Something tells me I'd better not come to your house when your father's around. We're going to have to sneak around if we want a peaceful life." The tone of his voice had grown more serious as he tacked on that last observation. Her eyes locked with his. His remarks implied that they would be seeing a lot of each other. The prospect of seeing him again and again sent a charged feeling of excitement shooting through her veins.

"Until I can find some way of getting him to change his opinion about you, I guess you're right. It probably would be better if I didn't mention that I was seeing you. We'll have to have some kind of signal on the telephone." She laughed, shaking her hair out of her eyes, and then continued. "You know something? He still won't tell me why he dislikes you. Did you just rub each other the wrong way or was it one specific incident?" Nicole narrowed her eyes as she shot the question at him. She watched his profile closely, and it was just as she expected. The lean angles and planes of his face seemed to close up. When he looked toward her, his silvered eyes dragged her into them with their sudden intensity.

"He'll tell you one of these days. Mark my words."

He turned his head to check the light, which was changing to green. He dragged the gearshift into position with a powerful thrust, giving more force to his words. The car shot forward. The light flickering through the trees and into the windows played across the hard angles of his face but gave nothing away. What he didn't want her to know he kept hidden.

But his continuing reticence made her feel more and more uneasy. This compelling enmity between her father and Jake disturbed and intrigued her and loomed large in her mind, and obviously Jake wasn't going to throw any light on the subject. She watched him pensively for a moment and then dragged up another topic that was gnawing at the back of her mind.

"Do you see other women besides me?"

He saw immediately through her forced attempt at passing interest. "Would you believe me if I said no?"

"Not really," she said in an airy tone.

"Are you jealous?" he taunted her softly.

"No, just curious. Why would I be jealous? I have no claim on you."

"You're jealous, all right, of the idea that there might be others," he asserted. "I can see it burning in those catlike green eyes."

"Well, you don't have to sound so pleased about it," she retorted waspishly.

He laughed deep in his throat as he turned the car onto a small side road. "If it's any consolation to you, I can't stand seeing you with that stiff-necked attorney, either. I don't like thinking of him with his hands on you." He slipped the words in quietly with stunning effect. The waves of golden pleasure pooling inside her were undeniable.

The car pulled into a wide yard. A large warehouse loomed up in front of them. In the nearby marina, gleaming white boats lined the docks. Jake switched off the ignition.

"How did you ever find this place? Is it safe at night?" she wondered aloud.

"I've got a top-of-the-line security system." They got out of the car, slamming doors simultaneously, then walked toward a wide yawning entrance to the warehouse. With open curiosity she looked up at the imposing structure. Inside, the warehouse was cool and dimly lit. They moved toward a caged elevator used to transport goods from one level to another.

"Do you own the warehouse?"

"The bank owns it. I rent out space and the income pays the mortgage. I had the loft converted into an apartment for myself. If I ever move, I can rent that, too." She shot him a sideways appraising glance. Some of his father's expertise in real estate had definitely rubbed off onto the son. She didn't voice her thoughts.

"So this is the quintessential bachelor pad. This is where you lure unsuspecting young women. To have your way with them?"

"I wouldn't describe any of them as being unsuspecting." His eyes mirrored the dry humor in his words. Nicole flushed, thinking that his words could easily apply to her.

"At least I don't have to pick a number and wait in line." Her tone of voice was glib, but it didn't mask the fact that she didn't like being one of many. Even though she had no real claim on Jake, jealousy surged inside her again, as strong as the look of possession she saw in his eyes. The strength of that jealousy dismayed her. Never before had she realized how potent the emotion could be. It was like a sleeping tiger, dormant inside a person, springing to life with ferocity when aroused.

Jake shoved aside the elevator's wire door and they stepped inside. He closed the door, and the elevator started on its ascent with a jolt, catching Nicole off balance. His hands shot out and he caught her, bringing her close to him. Looking steadily into his eyes, she felt his hands tighten around the soft skin of her upper arms. The wire elevator cranked to a stop, and, sliding back the bolt, Jake released the lock. The wire mesh door slid back and they stepped out. A few feet beyond there was another door, which Jake unlocked. They entered a large, open-plan apartment.

A handsome spiral staircase joined one level of the loft to the next. Nicole turned slowly, surveying the top level. From where she stood she could see an unmade king-size bed. Clothes and books were tossed around with no attempt at neatness. Empty coffee cups and the occasional beer can dotted the room. Newspapers littered the sofa and tables.

His gaze followed hers. "No one has ever accused me of being obsessively neat," he remarked.

"It looks like a bachelor's paradise," she remarked dryly, dropping her handbag onto a nearby chair. Their eyes locked as they smiled at each other in silent amusement.

She turned her attention back to the apartment, taking in the gray carpeting on the floors and the lofty open-beamed ceilings. The sun streamed through tall narrow windows, casting sweeping shafts of light across the floor. Off to one side was a small kitchen. On the opposite side of the room near the windows a dark brown leather sofa and chairs were placed near some built-in bookshelves. Lamps and tables completed the picture.

"Nice," she murmured. "Do you spend any time here?"

"Not a lot. Want a drink, while I shower and change?"

"No thanks," she called over her shoulder as she drifted toward one of the windows. When she looked down she could again see yachts moored in neat white rows in the marina below. Turning around again, she discovered he had disappeared up the spiral stairs. Her gaze wandered around the room haphazardly.

"Have you ever thought seriously about moving out of your father's house?" His voice echoed down from up above.

"Lots of times, but I never do anything about it. I've been thinking about moving out even more lately. You see how my father is—he tries to run my life. I really need my own place."

"It would be nice if I could call you without having the phone slammed down in my ear," he said.

She smiled to herself. She could hear the shower start to run. She blotted out the images her mind threw up of a naked and wet Jake, and walked over to the bookshelves. She saw some photographs in gilt frames that aroused her curiosity and lifted one. It was hard to believe that Jake had ever been young. All that overpowering masculine confidence and charged sensuality so near the surface made it difficult to imagine him as a vulnerable child.

But when she peered closely at the photograph she knew without a doubt that the lanky youth with the laughing eyes and thick rumpled hair had to be Jake. Equally so, the man next to him had to be his father, they were so similar in appearance. They had obviously been fishing and were both holding up their catch. Jake's father had taken a stance that demonstrated his exasperation that his son had hooked a grouper of considerable size, while he was holding up his own catch—a miserable pint-size yellowtail snapper.

She put the photo down as a sense of vulnerability shot through her. Once again she wondered why she had agreed to go out with Jake. But, gazing appreciatively around at his home, seeing how he lived, examining his possessions, picking up photographs like this one, only enhanced her growing feelings for him. In spite of her confused feelings about Jake, she liked what she saw. He appeared to come from a solid background with many of the same values she possessed. There were many things about him she admired. She already knew she was strongly attracted to him, more than to any man she had ever met before. Restlessly she looked around, unwilling to get on that emotional seesaw again. Her glance strayed to another photograph.

It was a picture of a woman, a beautiful woman with a beautiful smile. She had a heart-shaped face and long hair pulled neatly into a French twist. From the fashions and makeup, Nicole could tell that the woman wasn't one of her contemporaries. The picture had been taken twenty-five or thirty years ago. She wondered if it was Jake's mother or some other close relative. Wandering farther down the line of shelves she discovered some trophies. Reading the brass plaques, she learned that Jake had won them for the swimming team in college. The shelf above held some books on fishing. She examined them briefly and put them back. These were all attractive facets to his personality. Absentmindedly she turned back to the woman in the photograph, wondering once again who she was. But she had no more time to wonder.

A sudden movement made her turn around with a slightly guilty start—she had been caught spying. Jake, broad shouldered and fresh from the shower, loomed over her with an expression in his eyes that confirmed what she felt. Clad only in a pair of trousers, he stood drying his hair with a thick towel. He had been watching her. He roped the towel around his neck, and the biceps in his arms flexed menacingly. His gray eyes narrowed. She didn't know how long he had been standing behind her. She didn't remember hearing the shower stop, she had been so absorbed by the photographs and trophies.

"Find something interesting?" He moved closer with that powerful stealthy animal grace that was so integral to his personality. Her heart drummed inside her. For the first time she was acutely aware of being alone with him in an isolated place. The heady excitement throbbed through her veins, and her blood ran hot as she stared at his naked chest. Trying to cover up the impact of his surprise appearance, she turned back to the photographs.

"I was just looking at these. Is this you and your father?"

He moved closer to her so that only inches separated them. His nearness stole her breath away. She felt trapped. Out of the corner of her eye, she saw a rogue bead of water sliding over the hairs on his forearm. She couldn't drag her eyes away. He stood close behind her, completely uninhibited by his state of semidress, with typical male disregard for such things. He lifted the frame and focused his attention on it.

"That was taken when I was about twelve. My father lives over in Fort Lauderdale now." Nicole's ears picked up the underlying threads of deep affection in his tone. "It used to really please him when I outdid him at something. But he never wanted me to get a big head, so he used to hide his pleasure whenever I succeeded in outdoing him and pretend to be really ticked off." He put the picture back down on the shelf.

Nicole's eyes held a mischievous glint, but she managed to keep a straight face and solemn expression when she replied, "Do you think he succeeded in keeping you from getting bigheaded?"

A bemused smile lifted one corner of his mouth as he flicked a sideways glance at her. He lowered his head so that he was breathing in her scent while his hands rested on her waist. "Not entirely," he admitted with slow disarming candor.

His nearness was devastating her composure. Waves of sensation heated and electrified her skin, sending thousands of sensuous darts through her limbs. It was impossible not to acknowledge that she would like nothing better than to run her hands over his sleek, taut, tanned skin, to feel the flex of shoulder blades underneath her fingers and to run her fingers down the hollow of his spine to his hard waist, where dark trousers hung precariously on narrow hips. Out of a sense of self-preservation more than curiosity she turned to the other picture.

"Who's the woman?" she asked, tipping her head to one side speculatively, inching away at the same time.

The minute the question hung in the air, the atmosphere underwent a subtle change. The photograph locked his attention, but he didn't lift it with the same affectionate regard as the other one. Instead he looked down at it with an enigmatic expression. Jerking the towel from around his neck, he pulled it all the way off before replying to the question, as if he were somehow distancing himself from it.

"That was my mother. She died when I was about sixteen."

"She was very pretty."

"That's the way I like to remember her." His tone was so flat, so dismissive and so completely discouraging, it forced her to drop the subject and not ask any more direct questions about his mother. Her death must have been a loss he didn't like to talk about.

She decided on another tack. In a way their loss was a common bond. "My mother died when I was much younger, too. As I told you, my father raised me with the help of his sisters. Did you ever find yourself wishing your father would remarry?"

"Not that I can remember. I was almost grown when she died. By that time, I had discovered girls. It wasn't a mother I was needing." She turned in time to catch the wry twist of his mouth and the gleam in his eyes.

"What about your father? Wasn't he ever lonely? Didn't you ever want him to marry again?"

"My father and I always got along well. He didn't interfere too much in my life and I didn't interfere in his. I never thought much about him finding someone else because I was too wrapped up in my own interests at the time—sports, college, eventually police work."

Once again his tone had been dismissive. The look in his eyes was meant to shake her off. When Jake didn't want to talk about something, it was like a metal door clanging shut in front of your eyes. She remembered her own words about having to find out about him for herself. Now he wasn't any more revealing about himself than when she had first gone out with him.

"I always wished my father would marry again," she announced pensively, "but he never did."

"What about women friends? Didn't your father have any of those?" Jake's features hardened speculatively. A strange needling tone that puzzled her entered his voice.

"None that I know of," she replied, turning to look at him. Still close behind her, Jake's body almost touched hers.

"Maybe he keeps his women well hidden, conveniently tucked away. He could have had several mistresses that you never even knew existed." The wry twist of his mouth altered the lean hollows of his cheeks, but it wasn't remotely like a smile.

"Quite honestly, I don't think he's the kind of man to keep a mistress," she said defensively. "I think there have been women from time to time, but he never found someone that he cared deeply enough about who could take my mother's place. That's why he never married again."

"Maybe he never wanted to get involved deeply again. Maybe he just wanted to fool around."

He was forcing her to defend her father. At first she didn't understand this vague needling attack Jake was engaging in, but then she reminded herself that there was no love lost between Jake and her father.

"No, I don't think so." She watched the features of his face harden at her continued denial.

"It's dangerous to put people on pedestals, Nicole. They have a way of falling off."

"I'm not putting him on a pedestal. I'm sure he's gone out with other women from time to time. He's no saint. The point I'm making is that he never found anyone special enough to take my mother's place."

Suddenly, her words brought back a distant faded memory. "Now that you mention it, I do remember overhearing a conversation between my aunts one time. They thought there was someone. It was not long after my mother died. He must have been very lonely, but the affair must have burned out, because nothing came of it. Passionate affairs have a way of doing that. Don't they?" she remarked pointedly.

Looking deep into each other's eyes, they both knew the conversation had undertones applying to their smoldering relationship. They both knew they were poised on the brink of something tricky; what was happening between them could easily blaze with blinding brightness and just as easily burn itself out.

"There are always exceptions to every situation." His hand touched the side of her face. "Whether or not romances last, there's something inevitable about them. I've seen even the more intelligent people tell themselves a relationship won't work, that this isn't right or that something else makes the relationship an impossible one, but they go ahead with it anyway."

A shudder ran through her. He couldn't have put it any more plainly. She covered his hand with her own, while her gaze was absorbed into his. The contact was electric. Her warm palm felt the fine hair on the back of his hand as if it were acutely sensitive to each strand.

"Aren't you going to finish dressing?" Her voice had a disturbed edge that she couldn't hide. "I'm starving."

"So am I," he quipped. Lazy sensuality rolled into his eyes, and she knew he wasn't referring to food.

When Jake returned he was neatly groomed in a dark lightweight business suit that underscored his deeply tanned rugged good looks. A pearl-gray shirt picked up the silver cast of his eyes. Long tanned fingers adjusted a maroon-and-black-striped tie. Nicole watched appreciatively. At the same time she wondered fleetingly if she couldn't somehow promote some goodwill between her father and Jake. They were both reasonable, intelligent men. There had to be a way for them to overcome past differences. Jake moved alongside her, propelling her toward the door.

"Maybe I should invite you over for dinner one evening, so that you and my father can get to know each other."

He paused before opening the door, looking down at her. "That's an appealing idea. You want to know why it appeals to me? Because it would be interesting to see which one of us came out of it alive." He kept a straight face, but black humor danced in his eyes.

Nicole had the feeling that he meant every word. Jake was a puzzling personality. One minute he was full of teasing sensuality, the next full of hard-bitten cynicism, and he was capable of making quicksilver changes from one to the other with infinite ease. But she couldn't deny the powerful aura of charged excitement that he was weaving around her. She attempted to reason away the disturbing cynicism. A man couldn't help getting that way in the line of work Jake was in, always dealing with the dark side of the human experience. But it left her feeling uneasy for a few moments.

They descended in the elevator. Jake changed the subject to what she had mentioned before, getting a place of her own. "Let me know what you're looking for. If you decide to move into a place of your own, I might be able to help."

She turned to him with a questioning look. "Do you really mean that?"

"Every word. Remember, I've got good connections in the business because of my old man."

"How come you never went into real estate?" she asked.

"It didn't appeal to me as a means of earning a living. And when I was graduating from college, a recruiter from the police force visited the campus to discuss careers in police work. We had a long talk, and I was instantly hooked. When I got out of college I decided to try it. There was all the excitement and the fascination of the criminal mind, putting together the pieces of a crime. It's often painstaking, tedious work but I like hunting down a criminal and bringing him in—it's very satisfying after months of hard work. My job is what broke up my engagement—she wanted me to give it up. I will never give it up voluntarily." His words shot through her with reverberating force. He was saying in effect, for her benefit, *I'm a homicide detective. That's what I am. That's what I'll always be.* She gazed back at him in silence. When he opened the car door she slid inside noncommittally.

They spent all afternoon and evening together. It was as if they didn't want to leave each other. They had two meals out, though Nicole barely remembered eating. She lost all sense of time when she was with Jake. They talked and laughed easily together, completely absorbed in each other.

When he brought her home, it was very dark and very late. They both got out of the car, but before she could move away, he trapped her against the side of it. Resting his hands on her shoulders, he lowered his head and teased her mouth with his, lightly grazing her lips with a succession of kisses until he felt her answering response. Then he kissed her in earnest. Kissing Jake was like being engulfed by a sensual storm; he held little back. His mouth burned hers, his hard thighs pressed through the thin material of her dress. He consumed her with an urgency and passion that blinded her to everything around her, filling her with a fiery need that matched his.

The heated exchange was becoming more and more arousing until finally she pulled away. His hands tightened and held on to her for a reluctant moment. She murmured a ragged good-night and pushed out of his arms, starting to make a move for the door, to escape with what was left of her self-control. Suddenly, a car door slammed, the sound echoing down the deserted street. Nicole turned her head in the direction of the sound to see Richard jogging across the road, his tie flapping against a white dress shirt. In a blinding flash, she remembered that Richard had called earlier in the week, wanting to speak to her in person, and that she'd agreed to go out tonight for dinner. Sagging back against the car, she realized that it had completely slipped her mind. Ever since she and Jake had lunched yesterday, all thoughts of anything else but Jake had vanished from her mind. Remorse haunted her eyes.

Jake's voice penetrated her stunned mind while his gray eyes drilled into hers. "What is he doing here?"

"I had a date with him. I completely forgot about it." There wasn't even a plausible excuse she could summon up. "I recently ended our relationship, and Richard wanted to talk about it."

She felt so ashamed of herself. It had never been her intention to treat Richard shabbily. She turned around to face the music.

Richard stopped dead when he recognized Jake. Barely a yard separated the three of them. A man of grace and polish, Richard rarely lost his patience, but now Nicole watched it slipping away.

Richard ignored Jake, and grabbed hold of her arm. Reining in his temper, he focused his eyes on Nicole's face. "I thought we had a date tonight, Nicole," Richard said loudly.

"I . . . uh—" she began, but suddenly couldn't find her voice.

Jake stood silently at her side, but she sensed coiled anger building inside him. Taller and more ruggedly built than Richard, he had the psychological edge of physical strength coupled with his considerable experience at taking charge of potentially explosive situations. He loomed over her and Richard.

Richard's strident tones must have carried in the humid night air. The lights flashed on at the side of the front door, then the door swung open. Nicole's father's silvered head was haloed by the hall light.

"What the hell is going on out here?" As soon as her father saw Jake, he pinned his daughter with steely blue eyes.

"We're having a friendly little discussion, Mike. Maybe you'd like to join in the fun." Jake's insolent tones rolled into the tense, highly charged atmosphere. Her father's gaze stayed riveted on her face.

"I told you to stay away from this bastard. Nothing I say counts with you where he's concerned."

Torn between loyalty to her father and the strong growing attraction to Jake, Nicole couldn't answer. The knowledge groaned inside her, that the attraction to Jake had become the ruling factor in her life. One look at the calculating look in Jake's eyes said that he was very much aware of that fact, too. It was slowly coming home to Mike Bradley as well but with a much different reception.

Jake continued to challenge her father with the lazy insolent message in his eyes. Leaning against the side of his car, he was savoring every minute. His whole attitude was designed to enrage her father even more, Nicole realized. She felt a sense of helplessness stealing over her. Being caught in something over which she had no control had a dizzying effect on her. Before the situation deteriorated any more, she tried to sidestep it. "Why don't we call it a night, before we become the evening's entertainment for the whole neighborhood."

But her father wouldn't budge, his eyes were riveted on Jake's face, gleaming with some nameless fixation. Palpable, intense, mutual dislike hung between them. Their tempers seemed near the flash point. She tried to reason the situation away as two pigheaded men clashing over some long-past disagreement, but deep down she sensed it was much more than that. She knew she was going to have to find out for herself whatever it was. She held her breath, not knowing what was coming next.

"I'm going to get even with you for this, Slater—" Nicole watched her father's finger jab at the air "—if it's the last thing I do."

"If there's any evening of scores to be done around here, Mike, I think I'm the one who should be doing it." The quiet threat packed a lot of punch.

Taut muscles worked in Nicole's father's jaw. There was plenty he wanted to say, but something kept him from saying anything at all. Since she couldn't get her father to budge an inch she turned and appealed to Jake. "If you care anything about my feelings, will you please go?"

But Jake and her father continued to stare at each other as if she didn't exist. The startling realization that the enmity between her father and Jake was stronger than Jake's feelings for her leaped in front of her eyes, cutting her to the quick.

Richard stood sullenly on the sidelines watching and assessing with his lawyer eyes. Finally he added his own observation. "You're not a popular guy around here, Slater."

Like a big sleek wildcat, handsome, hypnotic and powerful, Jake turned on him in a flash. He looked as if he was itching for a fight, but he let Richard's words go. Nicole appreciated Jake for that.

"Richard, I'm sorry—especially for forgetting about tonight. But I thought I made my feelings clear. We can't see each other anymore." She hadn't wanted to put it so bluntly in front of everybody; she'd wanted to talk more to him about it in private. But the situation demanded that she declare her feelings once and for all in front of everyone.

Richard stared at her for a long decisive moment. "I won't take up any more of your time," he said, then headed for his car.

For a moment there was silence between Jake and her father, as if her words had had some kind of salutary effect. But Nicole knew that was not the case and she also knew that she had had enough. She couldn't take much more.

Turning away to go into the house, not caring if they tore each other apart, she sensed Jake's gaze on her back. He called out to her, making her pause. "I'm sorry about all this, Nicole. Good night."

His words brought some comfort. At least for a moment he had put aside his hostile feelings toward her father to consider hers. Swinging around to gauge the sincerity of his words, she saw the old reckless, unrepentant dangerous charm return. "I'll call you," he added, and the look in his eyes promised that he would see her again. Then he walked away without looking back. She could still feel the touch of his lips on her mouth from when he had kissed her earlier.

With a shaky sense of relief she walked inside. She heard her father following her, slamming the door behind him. Once inside her bedroom, she sank onto the bed, deciding on one thing. Tomorrow she would start hunting for a place to live. She was definitely moving out as soon as possible. She was never going to be subjected to the humiliation of another encounter like the one she had experienced this evening.

* * *

On Sunday morning, while her father was out playing golf, Nicole scoured the newspapers and then went to look at a few places that could be viewed on a Sunday. The ones she looked at were either awful, but affordable, or very nice, but terribly expensive. Discouraged and dispirited she returned home, kicked off her shoes and sank onto the sofa. When Jake telephoned later in the day to ask her out, she told him that she had been out looking for a place of her own. Jake immediately suggested a condo that was available, and said he would come by in an hour and they could take a look at it. When she announced that her father could return from golfing anytime, Jake informed her that he would wait outside. She hung up the phone with a smile curving her mouth. After a good night's sleep, she had more or less convinced herself that Jake and her father were just two extremely obstinate males, and neither one was willing to bend.

Her father hadn't come home yet when Jake arrived. He was leaning against the car as she came out the door, watching her with that lazy, enigmatic gleam in his eyes and the intense absorption that characterized everything he did. There was a smile on his face when he rolled away from the car and walked up the path to meet her.

"I see the coast is clear."

"He's still out playing golf."

"What made you suddenly decide to look for a place of your own? Was it only because of last night?" His eyes probed the depths of hers, as if he were looking for some kind of sign. "Did it have anything to do with me?"

"In a way," she conceded. "I've been thinking of moving out on and off for a long time. But it's my father's attitude toward you that's been the deciding factor. I don't want the hassle we had last night to repeat itself every time you come around to take me out or every time you call on the telephone." She knew her admission reflected her acceptance of the fact that she expected to be seeing a lot of him.

"That makes two of us." He grinned enigmatically.

He opened the car door and she slid inside. When he sat behind the wheel she studied him for a few moments, watching his movements with a sidelong glance. There were times when she sensed a duality about Jake. Moments when he threw up some kind of smoke screen over what little he showed of himself to the world. It was moments like this, when he was completely unfathomable, silent and enigmatic, that she wondered if she would ever really know him at all. But she reminded herself of other times when she sensed she was very near to discovering what she wanted to know about him.

When they reached the condo, Nicole couldn't believe her luck. Jake's description wasn't exaggerated. The neighborhood was pleasant and well maintained. The condo itself looked immaculate from the outside. She stood beside Jake at the front entrance as he unlocked the door, then they stepped inside.

Her spirits rose even higher as he propelled her through a small foyer into an open living room that ran the length of the condo. The entire apartment was

white, with white draperies and pearl-gray velvet-pile
carpeting throughout. Sliding glass doors opened at
one end onto a small, intimate patio. Off to one side
of the living room was a master bedroom and dressing room and bath. The furniture was walnut with
clean solid lines. On the other side of the main room
was a small kitchen and eating area. With bubble sky-
lights in the ceiling, daylight poured into the apartment, making it immensely appealing to the eye. Jake
pointed out that a parking bay ran underneath the
complex. He mentioned the rent, which was within her
price range. It was a gem set into a part of Miami that
remained desirable and conveniently near her office.
She swung around bemused.

"How did you find out about it?"

"A friend of mine owns the condo and asked me to
rent it for him while he's away working overseas. He
wanted someone who wouldn't wreck it, someone reliable. You look pretty trustworthy and reliable to
me."

"What about the furnishings?"

"He was going to put everything into storage, but I
convinced him to rent it out like this, that it would be
more profitable for him."

She sensed his eyes on her, watching and waiting for
her reaction. She gazed around enchanted. Partially
furnished, the condo solved all her problems immediately. Even if she could only get a short-term lease,
she could live here until she found something else. It
would give her the opportunity to look around at her
leisure and not be forced into taking something she
didn't want out of necessity. It was almost too good to
be true.

"How soon would I be able to move in?" she asked, trying to contain her mounting enthusiasm. Suddenly, she eyed him skeptically. There might be some hitch that hadn't been mentioned, she realized. But Jake's steady gaze and calm words allayed those fears.

"As soon as you want to. There's no lease. You pay the rent directly into this account." He reached into his pocket for a slip of paper and handed it to her.

After reading it, she lifted her gaze. "When is your friend coming back?"

"He's got a two-year contract with a major oil company. He just left last month. So you've got almost two years to stay here if you want to." Once again she couldn't believe her luck.

After a second look around, they drifted out. Jake locked the door behind them, and they went on to a restaurant for a late lunch.

When he brought her back to her house they both relaxed when they saw that her father's car was not out front. He noted their mutual reaction with a smile on his face, then turned and asked about the condo. "Do you think you're going to take it?" His expression was veiled, his face was partially in shadow.

"I doubt that I could find anything that would suit me better than this. I don't know how to thank you."

"My pleasure," he announced with a disturbing glint in his eyes.

Chapter 7

On Monday Nicole was back at work in the newsroom. The hectic pace of newspaper journalism
sometimes wore her out, but she loved it. She loved
racing to meet a deadline with the adrenaline kicking
in, forcing her to be single-minded. In the newsroom,
even with phones buzzing and people talking, the atmosphere went from indolent to concentrated to
charged as the deadline drew closer each day. It was
still morning, and she wasn't pushed yet. She had been
on the phone all morning checking out leads, putting
together the pieces to yet another puzzle, making a
story come alive.

Pausing from her work for the moment, she gazed
around idly. There were computer terminals everywhere, sleek desks and new carpeting. The newsroom
had been given a face-lift not so long ago. The offices
of the city editor, the assistant managing editor and

the managing editor were enclosed completely or behind glass partitions. The ones belonging to the assistant managing editor and the managing editor were elegant. The copy editors, reporters and photojournalists all had desks like hers in the open-plan newsroom. She leaned back in her chair, thinking once again about the condo. She had checked with the real estate agency and they had confirmed all Jake had told her about its availability and the rent. A small smile of satisfaction curved her mouth. She had definitely decided to take it and move out this coming weekend.

Last night, she had lain awake thinking about it, excitement at having her own place eddying inside her. For a few uneasy moments, she thought there might be some invisible strings attached to the offer, but after she checked it out, her mind had been put to rest. Sometimes, that enigmatic gleam in Jake's eyes when he became silent and uncommunicative made her feel that she didn't know him at all, and she wondered if she should trust him. In spite of the strong attraction she felt pulling her inexorably toward him, always in the back of her mind were the puzzling doubts associated with her father's reaction to him. No matter how she tried to reason them away, they remained. With another pang of uneasiness she realized there was something about Jake that was elusive, an untamed predatory quality, something there that she could never put her finger on but she knew it was there.

On Saturday, in order to avoid a confrontation with her dad, Nicole waited until he had gone to play golf and then moved her things out. With everything packed into the back seat and trunk of her car, she then took a moment to enjoy the beautiful Florida day. The sensation of starting out on a whole new lifestyle filled her. She left a note on the kitchen table explaining to her father that she was moving into a place of her own. Knowing his volatile temperament, she knew it was better to present him with a fait accompli, let him explode and then allow him a cooling-off period. When he'd had a chance to get used to the idea, she would call him to give him her new address and telephone number. He would probably come over to see her, take a look around the place and in his own inimitable way tell her exactly what he thought of it.

After stopping by the real estate agency to pick up the key, she let herself into the condo. In spite of its being furnished, there was lots to do. There were clothes to put away, sheets to put on the bed, all her personal possessions to arrange and shopping to do to stock the cupboards. The telephone was already hooked up and the electricity had been switched on during the week. She put her suitcases in the bedroom and arranged boxes full of books and compact discs near the shelves in the living room, then walked into the kitchen. Looking around at the empty shelves she decided that her top priority was a trip to the supermarket. She could finish unpacking any time in the evening, and she had all of tomorrow. With that thought in mind she sank onto the sofa to make a list of groceries.

The supermarket was jammed with Saturday shoppers. Music filled the air and the sound of cash registers mingled with voices. Absorbed by the task, she made her way around the market. Thoughts of Jake and her father crept into her mind. The intense enmity had flashed between them like some living thing. She felt caught up in it somehow. Yet when she had tried to find out why they felt that way, she had met with stony silence. Jake's reaction on the beach to her questions, the taut regard, the low clipped, charged responses had warned her off. The open hostility that was palpable made her wonder now more than ever what lay at the source of such charged emotions. She couldn't come up with any answers. The two people who could supply them weren't talking.

Her mind was so occupied by these thoughts that she didn't even remember piling her cart high with groceries. Concentrating on the task at hand, she went to find the nearest checkout counter.

Brown grocery bags lined the small kitchen along with boxes of canned goods and cleaning supplies. It was so crowded that Nicole had to step over things to get from one side to the other. Before she tackled putting them away, she decided to change her clothes, feeling hot and sticky from the trip to the supermarket.

A short time later she emerged from the bedroom tying an old white shirt into a knot at her waist. Faded jeans outlined her long legs and spanned her hips and thighs like a well-worn glove. She ran her hands through her shoulder-length hair, tossing it away from her face, wondering what to tackle first.

A knock at the door interrupted her again. Stepping gingerly around and over groceries, she went to open it. "Who is it?" she demanded.

"It's me, Jake." The low-pitched reply triggered an instant flood of emotions. The opening door revealed silvered eyes cast in a curious but thorough assessment of her, his lean face slightly angled downward, the powerful, muscled frame in a characteristic stance of impatience. Charged male vitality flowed from him. One hand, clutching a police radio, was braced against the doorjamb. He was working and had obviously taken the time out to stop by.

"Your legendary sense of timing is all off today. You couldn't have come at a worse time. I'm a mess and so is the kitchen." She twisted her head with a wry sidelong glance at the groceries littering the floor.

"You look good to me. Aren't you going to invite me in?"

Without another word Nicole stepped aside, watching him from underneath thick lashes. Like a caged animal Jake invaded the kitchen, filling up the space between them, easily dominating it with his restless force. She watched him place the police radio on the counter. He wore a deep blue business suit that spanned his shoulders, emphasizing their breadth, and a light blue shirt and striped tie. Pushing away the jacket, he propped his hands on narrow hips and peered down at her.

"I can't stay long. I just stopped by to ask you if you wanted to go deep-sea fishing with me tomorrow." His eyes narrowed speculatively on her face for a minute while he waited for her reply.

"Deep-sea fishing." Her eyes went curiously blank, then searched his, wondering what would be expected of her. She had never been fishing in her entire life, didn't know one end of a fishing rod from the other. He grinned down at her with reckless macho charm.

"I think you would like it. The currents are right and the marlin should be out there. It's really something to see a big game fish landed if you've never seen it before. Do you want to go?"

She wanted to be with him; she wasn't so sure about the rest of it. Cocking her head to one side she mulled it over, knowing she was ultimately going to say yes, but making him wait for her reply all the same. Jake's lethal gray-eyed stare ate her alive as his hand shot out and hooked around the curve of her neck, caressing it easily. His touch was like catnip on her senses, weakening her limbs. Dizzying arousal crawled down her legs and arms under the pressure of his nearness. But thoughts about the intense enmity between Jake and her father still hovered at the back of her mind, too. She still didn't have any answers. Now that they knew each other better, now that they had become more involved, the thought occurred to her that she stood a better chance of getting him to open up about it.

Pulling away from his hand she leaned back against the kitchen counter and folded her arms in front of her. Her whole attitude was both provocative and challenging as she crossed one long leg over the other with her head tipped to one side. Jake's eyes became instantly alert—he knew she was after something.

"I've never been deep-sea fishing before," she said slowly.

"There's always a first time for everything." His dry tone hinted that it wasn't necessarily deep-sea fishing he was alluding to. "I'll be the one doing all the work. A friend of mine will be driving the cruiser. You can sit around looking beautiful in something skimpy."

His eyes danced with a lazy sensuality that was highly erotic and contagious.

Surveying him slowly, letting the full play of her sensual side come out, Nicole decided to go for it. She wanted some answers and she had made up her mind to do a little pushing to get them. "It sounds like fun. I might go if—"

He cut in neatly. "What do you mean you *might* go if?" The lazy sensuality developed a fine edge.

"I'll go if you tell me what happened between you and my father. After the other night outside the house, seeing you two coming face-to-face with each other, I think you owe me an explanation. I'm beginning to suspect it's something far more serious than I first thought. Surely we know each other well enough that you can tell me now." Nicole watched a small muscle in the side of Jake's jaw flex ominously.

"That's between me and him. What brought this on? Why are you pushing me to find out? Why don't you push him?" For a moment their eyes dueled silently.

"I would much rather *you* told me." It was not only her fears that she wanted him to put to rest. All that was feminine inside her felt he should explain. In actuality she was putting his feelings to the test.

"Why would you rather I told you?" The terse question hung in the air between them.

"Because I want you to prove something to me," she said boldly.

"You're *telling* me I have to prove something to you?" Tipping his head back, he peered down at her from his lofty height. Everything that was male about him challenged her. His back was up.

Trying not to be intimidated, she hesitated, then continued calmly enough. "The other night I was caught in the middle of this ridiculous enmity you and my father insist on keeping alive. I got the feeling it was more important to you than whatever feelings you have for me. I want you to prove that what you feel for me is more important than some old grudge."

As he advanced toward her with that prowling animal grace, the kitchen diminished in size alarmingly. His retort came low, sure and swift.

"I'm beginning to think what I feel for you is more important than the grudge I have with your father. I'm beginning to think that the only obsession I have is the one standing in front of me."

"That's not good enough. I want an explanation— not a sidestepping evasion." Her insistence and the stubborn, proud tilt of her chin spurred him on.

"You want me to prove something to you. I'll prove something to you." The lazy sweep of his gaze dropped slowly over the swell of her breasts straining against the white shirt tied in a knot at her small waist, down to the flare of her hips and the apex of her thighs.

A husky tremor invaded her tone when she replied, "I don't want you to think that just because you helped me get this condo, that you can just walk in here whenever you feel like it and—"

"Grab you? Now why would you think a thing like that?"

"I wouldn't have taken this place if I thought there were any strings attached."

Trying to maintain some kind of poise, she made the mistake of looking deep into his eyes. Their glittering

depths shook her. Tantalized by her growing agitation, Jake reached out. Clasping the curve of her neck,
he forced her head closer, so that barely inches separated their lips.

"I'm trying to explain that I never agreed to anything," she continued, her words a breathy dead
giveaway that she realized the whole situation was
suddenly backfiring on her. Thoughts about the enmity between Jake and her father vanished instantly
from her mind. Jake's gaze dropped to her mouth.
With his hard thighs locking her against the cabinet,
he shrugged out of his jacket and tossed it impatiently aside. A fine trembling attacked her, vibrating
through her.

"You can't stop a man from thinking, Nicole."
Lowering his head, he breathed his next words against
her neck. "I'm here now. What are you going to do,
send me away like a naughty boy? Throw me out
bodily?"

"Your friend can have his condo back any time. I
can move out, just as quickly as I moved in." Feeling
like a nervous filly with an aroused stallion nosing
around, her retort was low, edgy and taut.

"Where will you go? Where will you run to?" His
tone suggested there was no escape. "You're too old
to run home to Daddy, and you can't find a place to
live at the drop of a hat." His hands rested on her
shoulders, his gaze dropped to the agitated rise and fall
of her breasts.

"You're driving me crazy, Nicole. You've got me
tied up in knots. You can't get me to stay away. It's too
late for that now." His gaze slid to her lips again. Her
mouth opened but no sound came out. His hard fin-

gers captured her jaw, needing no second invitation. Then his mouth claimed hers in a driving, possessive kiss. Shuddering under the power of her own desire Nicole melted under the blistering heat of their union, which transcended everything else. Drowning in sensation and held captive by his invasive rugged maleness, she breathed in his clean musky scent.

When he lifted his head his words fanned across her ear, with a mixture of rough tenderness. "Why don't you give in to me? It's what we both want."

Responding to the deep pull of his words, she slid her hands past his shoulders, and clasped his corded neck. Her mouth answered his. Their stifled sounds of mounting passion, the creak and groan of their bodies against the kitchen counter, the rustle of grocery bags filled the silence. Their legs pressed and mated as they tried to get closer to each other. His lips forced hers apart with a rough demand that fanned the heat building between them, while his restless hands arched her into him. Enveloped by his closeness, riding on a sensual high, Nicole felt a weakness attack her. Wise in the ways of arousing a woman, he urged her on, but soon it was not enough for either of them. Jake's hands swiftly and deftly untied the shirt. Groaning softly against his ear, she felt him flick open the front catch of her bra.

"Let me look at you." His husky words excited her as much as the touch of his hands. With her skin flushed, her eyes lazy with arousal and one hand curved around his neck, she leaned back against the counter, a beguiling mixture of brazen vulnerability.

As he pushed both bra and shirt aside, Nicole watched desire turn his eyes into molten silver. His quickening response to her female curves was inflammatory, but frustration was mingled with it because he knew he was fighting time. Any minute he could be called away. His narrowed drugged gaze slid from her lips down over her breasts in thorough inspection. She moaned softly with want. Not satisfied, hungry for more, he went for the zipper of her jeans. With a natural sultriness she didn't know she possessed Nicole leaned back against the kitchen counter, a willing victim to the sensual assault of his eyes and hands, drunk with the power she wielded.

"The damned radio is going to go off any minute." When he eased the faded jeans down slightly over the curve of her hips, his touch was electric on her bare skin. His powerful body shuddered, betraying his deepening arousal. He lowered his head and his mouth captured hers again. They kissed deeply. Breaking off the fiery full-blown kiss of passion, he buried his face in the soft curve of her neck, breathing her in.

"It's not enough," he groaned. There was no substitute for total possession; they both knew it. Even in the thick haze of her own desire Nicole sensed his control going. He made a rough sound deep in his throat and his hands encircled her hips and clasped her against him intimately. The hardening ridge of his manhood pressed hotly against her thigh. A fine tremor attacked her legs. The deep pooling ache of her growing arousal was turning her legs to rubber. Pressing her forehead against the side of his face, she felt intense waves of longing wash over her. She breathed his name on a ragged sigh. Desire pumped between them like a heady current. Male urgency screamed for release—nothing else mattered now. He started to lift her onto the counter. His low, thick command followed.

"Put your legs around me."

Nicole slid her hands across his broad, muscled back. Passion fused them together until her hand hit something cold, hard and made of metal. Instantly her mind identified it—the .38 revolver in the shoulder harness he always wore when working. Harsh reality struck back at her with full force as if ice water had been thrown at her face. It wasn't only the sensation of all that lean, rugged male strength and the promise it held that she was suddenly fighting against. It was what went with it. Her hands coming into contact with the cold metal gun brought it all back to her as nothing else could. Twisting her head away from his kiss, thrusting hard with her hands against his shoulders, she cried out.

"Stop. We've got to stop. This is crazy."

Suddenly raucous static sounds from the radio on the counter filled the kitchen. Relief swamped her as she realized that she had won a temporary reprieve. The dispatcher's voice announced an emergency, a 45, a corpse in Little Havana. Jake would have to go. His hands clamped spasmodically on her hips. With his head down and his eyes clenched tightly shut, he swore long and eloquently underneath his breath, and turned around. Dragging in his breath, he kept his back to her for a few moments. When he turned around, for a lengthening moment they stared at each other across the space that separated them. His narrowed eyes were alive with the knowledge that she had eluded him once again. He picked up the two-way radio and went out into the hallway saying that he would be answering the call right away. Nicole slowly refastened her jeans and her bra and retied her shirt. When he returned her eyes still glowed with a mixture of unsatisfied desire and relief.

"You're like a cat with nine sensual lives. We keep using them up one by one, don't we?" he noted evenly.

"I knew it would be like this for us if I let myself get involved with you," she shot back. Then she waited for him to say something in reply, knowing there was nothing either one of them could say. Long, long ago she had said she didn't want to get involved with a cop, and long, long ago he had said he couldn't be anything else. Stepping over bags, he reached the door and paused. Drugging desire fled and they returned to reality. With a sardonic flash of humor he pursued his original reason for being there.

"Before I got sidetracked by your...charms, I asked you if you wanted to come out deep-sea fishing with me. You still haven't answered me." They both knew she would be going. Putting conditions on her acceptance to his invitation had been a catastrophic failure.

"I'd like to go deep-sea fishing with you," she heard herself say. Nicole felt as if there was another person inside her over whom she had no control, doing her thinking, doing her answering, responding whenever he took her in his arms. Her wild heart ruled.

Chapter 8

The following morning Jake came by early to call for Nicole, as he'd said he would. Relaxed, he drove effortlessly down to the marina, sprawled behind the wheel of the Lotus Elan with one arm resting on the open window frame. Nicole scanned the passing scenery as the car shot down the road. But she was also very aware of the man beside her.

With mirrored sunglasses obscuring his eyes, a dark T-shirt stretched across his muscled shoulders and torso, and jeans that rode low on his hips, he was not diminished by casual clothes—far from it. The cool, calculating professional detective had been tossed aside with the three-piece suit. The quick, hard and dangerously compelling side of Jake was now exposed, his magnetic appeal increased.

Driving along, he explained his access to the yacht moored at the marina near the warehouse where he lived. "My father rarely uses it. Occasionally he takes some clients out on it to entertain them when he's putting together some kind of real estate deal. But mostly it just sits here. So he encourages me to use it whenever I get time off."

With screeching tires the car swung off the main road onto the side street that led to the marina. Nicole's long hair blew around her face. Noting the fluid grace of Jake's handling of the car, his quick reflexes, she speculated that he could have been a race car driver. He seemed to have that ability to apply himself with superlative ease to whatever he chose. She only wished it had been something other than being a cop.

. Not much later she and Jake and his friend Eric were aboard the motor-powered yacht, cruising out of the marina into deeper waters. Surrounded by a never-ending world of sea and sky, Nicole stood on deck admiring the view. Her eyes adjusted to the brilliant, dazzling tropical sunlight drenching everything around her. The yacht cruised past markers through safe channels until it was out in the open waters. Jake opened the throttle, and the cruiser shot forward. Instantly a joie de vivre, a sense of infinite freedom and a rush of wind enveloped them. Eric stood nearby, following a marine map and pointing at some dot on the horizon where the currents flowed and the marlin followed. In front of Eric, Jake's treatment of Nicole was almost impersonal, but when his friend disappeared below deck the hot flow of desire surged between them like a heady flame. He flashed a smile at her, which was intensified by the mirrored sunglasses concealing part of his face. Then he scanned the horizon. With one hand on the wheel he hooked the other possessively around her waist. Dressed in a brief white halter top and white shorts, Nicole felt the penetration of his lazy inspection even behind the sunglasses, and the curling deep response deep within herself.

The yacht sliced through the aquamarine waters of the Atlantic, continuing on its way toward the Gulf Stream. The warm current flowed from the Gulf of Mexico around the southern tip of Florida to the east coast, and then all the way north to Newfoundland. The migrating marlin followed it religiously.

By the time the cruiser neared its goal the sun was high in the sky. Stretched out on a recliner in the shade of the overhang of the top deck, Nicole dozed. Lulled by the gentle rock of the cruiser, she had almost fallen asleep. Suddenly excitement vibrated in the air. Eric shouted to her that Jake had a strike. From the cockpit where he was maneuvering the boat Eric pointed into the distance. Nicole sat up, straining to follow the direction of his hand. A bright silver flash caught her eye, and she recognized it as a giant fish. Her eyes followed it as it plunged beneath the aquamarine waters, disappearing again. Even in that short time the silver body and cobalt-blue spear of its bill and dorsal fin became etched into her mind. Leaving the recliner, Nicole moved near Jake, who sat with rod and reel. He was still gazing at the distant point that held her fascinated.

Strapped into the chair and pulling back on the rod, which was constructed to withstand hundreds of pounds of tension, Jake braced one long, leanly muscled leg against the transom and reeled in. Eric, still steering from the cockpit, glanced back over his shoulder, trying to get the cruiser into a better position.

Jake had to speak in a raised voice to make himself heard over the idling motors. "Watch. All marlin are tail walkers—they break for air when attacked."

Suddenly the fish exploded through the waters again. Leaping high in the air in a gyrating motion, the fish skimmed the surface on the broad fan of its tail so that it indeed appeared to be "walking." At the same time its large head flailed from side to side wildly trying to throw the hook. But it was a vain attempt.

"He's magnificent." Nicole's voice was filled with awe as the marlin dived beneath the surface again. The taut line of his rod whipped through the water, singing in the air as the great fish ran with it, plunging and coursing through the oceanic depths at forty to fifty miles per hour. Nicole's attention was equally divided between watching the fish's struggle for survival and watching Jake. The hard-bitten tenacity, the flex of biceps as he played the marlin on the long line, keeping the fish under control, giving it room to maneuver but still in control. Mesmerized by the unfolding battle, her gaze strayed to his hands, always so completely in control, whether they were driving a fast car, hauling in a huge fish or all over her.

Mirrored sunglasses hid the expression in his eyes, and the rest of his face gave away little. Strength, sureness and stamina were etched in his features. But it was his mouth, curved in a ruthless sensuality, that impressed her most while she watched the contest rage between man and wild creature. Both participants continued to vie for her attention. Her sympathy was divided equally at first. She wanted Jake to win; she wanted the fish to go free. But the more she watched, the more the silver flash of the fish and its valiant struggle for freedom won her sympathy, while the play of muscle in Jake's broad shoulders and the tops of his arms fascinated her. He kept pulling back on the rod, then always winding in, the movements repeated over and over again with monotonous regularity, as the match became not only one of superior intelligence pitted against strength and speed, but one of endurance and sheer grit on both sides. The minutes ticked away slowly for a half hour; the half hour turned into an hour. Finally the animal showed signs of tiring. When the silver body exploded from the water the spectacular leaps were no longer so flashy or so frequent. The sight saddened her even more, until she found it unbearable.

"Why don't you let it go?" she shouted. The words burst from her lips unchecked. "It's too beautiful to capture. Let me cut the line." The set of Jake's jaw only looked more adamant, with his mouth deepening at the corners. There was an empathy between them. He'd known where her sympathies lay long before the words escaped from her lips. The wry twist of his mouth confirmed it.

"Over my dead body, Nicole." Returning his attention to the singing line, he pulled back on the rod, then continued to wind in. The determination written on his face was exceeded only by his tenacity in hanging on to something he wanted.

After one hour and forty minutes she watched him claim victory. By then the fish was too weak to put up any kind of a fight at all. It was reeled in on the long line to the side of the cruiser. Nicole leaned indolently over the side of the yacht watching, saddened that something so wild and beautiful had been captured. Still alive and breathing, the marlin floated, quiescent in the waters lapping against the hull of the yacht as if it didn't mind being captured. Jake unwound his tall frame from the chair, walking over to where she stood.

"He's all worn out. You've defeated something wild and free and beautiful. What will you do now? Sell him to some Japanese restaurant and turn him into sushi?" Her taunting words challenged him.

"Maybe I'll stuff him and give him to you," he teased her, then leaned back alongside her. He was pleased with himself, pumped up with the satisfaction of having gotten what he was after. The look in his eye made her want to take some of the wind out of his sail.

"I don't know. Deep-sea fishing looks more like hard work than fun to me." Her tone was still accusing, implying he had perpetrated some kind of crime.

"You have to fight for what you want in life. But that doesn't mean that you can't have any fun while you're after it." Removing his sunglasses, Jake shot her a look full of innuendo. The sun had brought out the golden tones of her skin, and she looked bronzed and healthy. Her long hair was windblown around the soft contours of her face. The electricity between them was rampant.

He turned to locate Eric. Hailing him, he signaled that they would start hauling the fish in. Then he turned back to Nicole.

"Why don't you put on your swimsuit? We'll go for a swim."

A while later, in a black bikini, Nicole emerged from below deck. The first thing she noticed was that Jake had changed, too. The wide flare of his shoulders and the long hard legs were exposed by a brief black swimsuit spanning his narrow male hips. With his back to her, she watched the play of muscles, his shoulder blades undulating as he and Eric hauled in the marlin with the aid of pulleys and a net. Nicole walked over.

Lowered onto the gleaming teak deck, the fish was even more impressive close up. The three stood admiring the magnificent creature, which easily exceeded ten feet. Cobalt blue colored its long rounded spearlike bill and the dorsal fin that ran the length of its back. Knowing its impending doom the marlin watched them with its black feral eye. Both men stayed clear of the deadly bill. An unexpected lunge could impale. The marlin twisted and writhed as they hoisted it again to weigh it. The scale needle danced back and forth with the fish weighing in at 140 pounds, small for a marlin, but still an enviable catch for any sport fisherman.

Bemused, Nicole wondered why they did it, why the instinct to hunt and battle with something wild and free was so basic to man's instincts when it was no longer a necessity. More sympathy welled up inside her. Now life was oozing from the marlin. When she looked up, she caught Jake watching her.

"You still wish I had cut the line, don't you?"

"I think it's cruel. He was meant to roam the oceans, not end up as sushi or on a wall." She flashed him another challenging look. Checking to see that Eric had gone below deck so they were alone, she said what was on her mind without thought of the consequences.

"You know, I can't help remembering something Malcolm said to me that day we first met."

"What was that?" he asked with a dry look, knowing Malcolm.

"He said, 'Watch out for Jake, I think he's attracted to you. He'll hunt you down and pull you in like one of his prime suspects if you're not careful.'" She watched Jake's expression closely. He wasn't wearing sunglasses now, but the depths of his eyes were still unfathomable. But a telltale rigid stillness invaded his being. The lean, hard features of his face never budged.

"What's that supposed to mean? Am I supposed to cut the line on you, Nicole? Stop chasing after something I want? You ought to know me better than that by now." The words rolled from him with ease. But they splintered through her, striking an exposed nerve, effectively stunning her into silence.

Jake took the liberty of answering the question for her. "I won't cut the line," he announced quietly. The look in his eyes was as searing and dry as a desert wind. His look said he wanted it all. The hook had been set almost from the very first moment they met. She could fight, she could run, but in time she knew he would win. So did Jake.

With an air of bravado, she turned her back on him, walked slowly over to the side of the yacht, clambered down the swimming ladder, then plunged into the ocean swell.

The saltwater cooled her fevered mind and sunfevered skin. Jake plunged in after her. With powerful economic strokes he caught up with her and dragged her down by her legs, locking his arms around her waist to hold her in his embrace. Bubbles rose all around them as they floated slowly to the surface. Breaking through, Nicole gasped for air, twisted away from him, then swam in the other direction back toward the ladder. In moments he had caught up with her.

Clinging to the swimming ladder, she watched Jake surface in front of her. With water streaming down his broad shoulders, he shook his head and braced his arms on either side of the ladder, trapping her between them. Breathtaking harsh male vitality overstamped the powerful and ruthless set of his features. With his arms braced on the ladder, a fortress of sinewed strength surrounded her.

Jake gazed down at her. As she stood poised on the bottom rung of the ladder with her wet hair sleeked back from her face, her high cheekbones and catlike green eyes were accentuated. Jake absorbed them with an air of burning possession.

The air seemed to congeal around them into a heavy sensuality as the hunter moved in for the kill. Her chest was heaving from the exertion of the strenuous and futile attempt to stay ahead of him. Leaning her head back against the upper rungs of the ladder she tried to catch her breath, closing her eyes. When she opened them Jake's sensual mouth hovered inches from her own.

"I have a confession to make."

"About what?" she asked breathlessly.

"The condo you're living in."

"What about it?"

"It belongs to me. There is no man working over-seas."

Perplexity stilled her. "What?" she said in shock, riveted by the dominating force of his eyes.

"I wanted you away from your father, some-where..."

The penny clicked into a slot in her mind. She finished the thought for him. "Somewhere convenient. Why didn't you tell me before?"

"Because I didn't think you would take it, if I did."

"Oh, I might have taken it anyway," she said, turning her head away. "I seem to be destined to make a fool of myself where you're concerned. Besides, I don't think I would have gotten a better deal any-where else, do you?"

"No, I don't think you could." His lazy gaze examined her, his tone soft with a teasing merciless quality. It was just another way of telling her that he had her trapped, that he had outthought her and out-maneuvered her. Like the marlin, she was waging a losing battle and she might as well surrender. A bruised, wounded look surfaced in her eyes. Her tongue lashed out at him.

"You're still the same coldhearted bastard you were when I first met you. You don't give a damn about anything, least of all my feelings. I'm just another conquest to bolster up your macho image. There's no check on your appetites—you just go after whatever it is you want in life and take it. My feelings don't enter into it because this is all some kind of huge game to you.'' Hot tears stung her eyes, as she choked out the words. Cool matching beads of moisture slipped down her face. Jake's hardening features flinched visibly. Miraculously for a fleeting moment she touched something deep inside him.

He clamped his hand on her jaw, his reply low and heavy with deep running emotion. ''You've got it all wrong, Nicole, because I do care. The last thing I ever figured on was falling in love with you, but that's what's happened. I'm in love with you. Do you hear what I'm saying? No one is more surprised about it than I am, unless maybe it's you.'' A flash of sardonic amusement accompanied his words, as if fate had played a big joke on both of them.

Surveying him in silent wonder, Nicole thought this had to be the most unromantic way a man could choose to tell a woman he was in love with her. Dragged from him reluctantly as if it pained him to say it, tinged with regret and topped off by sheer male stubbornness to give in to it. The hard lines of his face drew closer. His silvered eyes scanned her face.

''If you didn't figure on falling in love, what did you figure on?'' she whispered with lips that trembled with emotion.

His expression went curiously blank, as if he were afraid she might see too much. Then he answered. ''I didn't figure on anything when I first met you, except that I had to have you. But when I went after you I got way more than I bargained for. You never figured on me either. Did you?'' he challenged softly.

Still fighting back hot tears, mute misery shining in her eyes, Nicole stared at this man who had the power to drag every kind of gut-wrenching response he chose from her with varying degrees of intensity.

He saw the sheen in her eyes and his whole manner softened; his hand caressed her neck. His voice took on a husky pitch. "Did you think I was kidding yesterday in the kitchen when I said you've got me tied up in knots?" He laughed with soft self-derision. "Pretty soon people will begin to talk about me. Whatever happened to Jake Slater, they'll say. He used to be a guy you could have a good time with. What happened to Jake?" With self-mocking humor he answered the question for her. Her waiting eyes searched his, his thumb caressed her lower lip teasing it. "Some hotshot reporter put a leash around him, that's what they'll say."

Hardly daring to believe what she'd just heard, Nicole watched breathlessly from beneath thick lashes, mesmerized by his touch. His hand moved stealthily along her shoulder. His gaze dropped to the deep cleft between her breasts. Seeing a rogue crystal droplet of water sliding into it, he lowered his head and caught it with his tongue, then kissed her breast. His hand slowly pushed the swimsuit strap off her shoulder, down her arm, to give him complete access. Her hand caught his wrist, a wrist of steel that would not be deterred.

"You got me," he whispered huskily. His gaze dueled silently with hers, daring her to stop him. "I've been chasing you, but you're the one who's hooked me, Nicole. It's not the other way around, honey. What are you going to do about it now that you've got me?" he taunted in low-pitched intimacy.

She closed her eyes. "I want more than you can possibly give," she breathed.

"How do you know what I've got to give if you don't give me a chance to give it?" Her hand was still locked around his wrist but the strap moved inexorably downward, until she felt the warm air on her exposed breast. The cool water had turned the nipple into a taut bud. But the touch of his hand turned it into a bud of desire. His words danced in her mind, sending powerful messages and responses through her body. She moaned softly. Her last shred of resistance faded, the warning bells of her instincts muffled by encroaching passion.

"I've got a key to the condo." He breathed the words against her ear. "I have to work late all this week but I want to come over after work on Friday. Will you think about it?" He gave her a moment to nod that she would.

His hand closed around the fullness of her breast gently, then he lowered his head until his mouth closed over the taut nipple. He teased and tugged and she pressed back against the swimming ladder, her foot still poised on the bottom rung, her back to the side of the yacht. When he lifted his head, his eyes were filled with raw desire. Then his mouth covered hers with a fiery possession. His tongue thrust deep inside. His hand slid to her hip, squeezing her bikini-clad hip. She felt the imprint of his hard thighs, the quickening of his body. Her silent protests went unheeded by her mind. But chance and circumstances were with her.

Suddenly Eric called to them from on deck. They broke apart guiltily, shaking with want, but the spell was broken. Nicole gasped as Jake tore his mouth away and took several deep steadying breaths. When they both looked up, Eric was hanging over the side, pointing to some clouds in the distance.

"Jake, it looks bad over there on the horizon. The radio says for all small craft to come in." He grinned at them with a knowing look.

"We'll be right up."

Swearing softly at himself, Jake shot her a dry look filled with male exasperation.

"How many of those nine lives have I used up? I'm beginning to lose count."

Chapter 9

On Monday morning in the newsroom Nicole's father finally caught up with her. She lifted the phone on her desk.

"My own daughter sneaks off like a thief in the night. Where the hell are you staying?" His voice shot over the wire.

"I left a note. There was no reason to worry." Deciding to take the bull by the horns, she told him about the condo.

"Well, I suppose I knew it would happen one of these fine days." He laughed with grudging resignation. "I'm sorry it came about the way it did. If it wasn't for that bastard, you would still be living at home. It's all his fault."

"Dad," she murmured, her gaze flicking around the newsroom, "let's not get into another heated discussion. Do you want my phone number and address? I'll be inviting you over for dinner soon but you can drop in anytime. You know I'll always be glad to see you."

"I guess I'll never see you anymore," he growled as she gave him the address and phone number, then started to make excuses about getting back to work.

"I'll come around after work to pick up some more of my things."

That evening when she went to her father's house, he greeted her at the door.

"I drove past your condo today. It's not bad. In fact it's very nice. How much are you paying?" His eyes narrowed when she mentioned the rent. His look of disbelief demanded an explanation.

"It's only temporary. The owner is working overseas on contract. He wanted to sublet it while he was away." She didn't dare tell him who the true owner was, not yet anyway. "Jake told me about it." She watched her father's face turn into stony disapproval at the mention of Jake's name.

"I should have known he had something to do with all this."

"Dad, you can't go on ignoring him forever. He's a fact of life." She walked through the living room with him and then into the kitchen, pausing near the sink.

"Meeting Jake has shown me how I really feel about Richard. I was never in love with him—we drifted into a relationship that was going nowhere. Jake stormed into my life and woke me up."

"I'll be happy when he storms out again," her father muttered, leaning back against the kitchen counter. "Tell me, Nicole. Were there any strings attached to this condo?'' He raised the question with a cynical gleam in his eyes.

''No,'' she lied smoothly. ''The owner wanted someone who would take care of the place and not abuse it or neglect it. Jake told him I would be an ideal tenant. He vouched for my character.''

''I'll bet he did,'' her father said pointedly.

Ignoring his innuendo she continued. ''Has anyone called? Are there any messages for me?'' She tried to sidestep the volatile situation. Her father appeared to accept her explanation with tight-lipped reluctance and didn't comment any further, except to tell her there were no messages.

After she had made a cup of coffee for them both she walked through the house to her old bedroom to pick up a few more of her things. When she came out, he stood watching her.

''Is everything working all right?''

''Everything is working fine. It's a great condo. Partially furnished, too. I couldn't ask for anything more.''

''Well, I could. I'd like to see that bastard staying away from you.'' Her father's temper flared again.

''Why do you dislike him so? He's done nothing to you.'' She watched her father's eyes grow flinty.

''It's what he would like to do to me. You don't know him the way I know him.''

She couldn't fathom what her father meant by that remark. But she had given up trying to wheedle out of him the reason for it. The closed expression on his face told her it was useless. The same went for Jake. She figured that sooner or later she would find out. It had to have something to do with their professional lives.

She guessed that somewhere along the line they had rubbed each other the wrong way, or possibly one had dropped the other in hot water. Whatever it was, it had left a lasting effect.

"What about that cold calculating bastard? Are you still going to see him?"

"Yes. I'm going to see him again." Her father's high-handed arrogance, his desire to control her life, were getting her back up. He had no right, just because of personal differences between him and Jake, to dictate who she should or shouldn't go out with socially.

"I thought you objected to his profession. I thought you never wanted to get involved with a cop."

"You're right. I've always promised myself that." Her voice echoed her own confusion, but her eyes flashed with green sparks. "If you want an explanation I can't give you one. Because I don't understand it any better than you do."

Her father tossed her a look that said he was slightly mollified by her words, but she thought she detected a deep concern in his eyes. The fact that he didn't elaborate on it only made her feel more uneasy about his continuing obstinacy. Inside she felt a guilty twinge because she knew she was teetering on the edge of getting deeply involved with Jake. She had only to think of the time in the kitchen and the day on the yacht, to know that things were progressing between them at breakneck speed. But she didn't want to alarm her father and arouse the famous Bradley temper. She had only just succeeded in getting him to accept the fact that she had moved out. Now was not the time to tell him that she wasn't at all sure about the role Jake was going to play in her life. She was only sure of one thing—she had fallen in love with him. And that had happened whether anyone liked it or not, including herself.

On Friday evening when Nicole was getting ready for bed the telephone rang. She picked it up with the uncanny feeling that it was Jake. The familiar tones of his voice rolled over the line.

"I'm at a pay phone. You've had time to think." The words echoed in her ear, making her heart pound and the blood roar through her veins. "There's no going back, Nicole. Where do we go from here? I want to come over—are you going to let me in?"

She closed her eyes, hoping fervently that she wasn't going to regret this decision until her dying day. "I want you to come over. I want you to stay, too." The soft note of surrender in her voice was unmistakable. The line became electrically charged as they both appreciated the depth of their feelings.

Jake's low-pitched voice was even lower than usual. "I'm not sure what time I'll get there. But I'll be there as soon as I finish. You can count on it."

"Okay." She put down the phone quietly, wanting to shake herself.

She walked into the bedroom and paced up and down for a while. There was a dull ache inside her. Something about her was incomplete and something inside her waited to be discovered. But the awful grinding longing that would not go away could not go on forever. She stripped off her clothes and got ready for bed. The clock ticked slowly. The hands seemed to move more slowly than usual.

She tried to read but ended up watching the hands of the clock move slowly around the dial. The hours crept by. She wondered what had happened to Jake. She'd have thought she would be on tenterhooks waiting, but sleepiness was stealing over her. Looking at the clock again, she decided he wasn't coming. A wry twist curved her mouth. When would she learn? This is the way it was, the way it would always be. What else could she expect from a homicide detective but broken promises, broken engagements? She tossed the book aside and turned out the light. When her head hit the pillow she fell almost instantly asleep, emotionally drained by the waiting and the disappointment. Deeper and deeper she slipped into sleep.

Stirring in her sleep, she turned over on her back. Lifting her arm out of the way, she flung it onto the pillow over her head. In some distant corner of her dream-soaked mind, she sensed a presence hovering high over the bed. A soft smile curved her mouth when the mattress sank slowly beneath the weight of the presence. The figure in the dark stood discarding his clothes with unhurried movements. It was a wonderful erotic dream and she moaned softly with pleasure. She wanted it never to end, and it was getting better all the time. Now the dark figure was bending over and kissing her. Warm, firm male lips brushed her mouth. Covers fell away from her bared shoulders. The warm possession of a phantom mouth trailed rhythmic, teasing kisses over the side of her face, her cheekbones, then down the side of her neck. She stretched lazily, giving her dream lover access. Like a cat with a thick bowl of cream she purred with pleasure. Shoes thudded on the floor. A zipper seared the silence.

More clothing joined the shoes, pelting the soft carpeting. Turning her head deeper into the pillow she sighed contentedly, but warm, hard fingers caught her chin, forcing her head around, then firm insistent lips claimed hers again.

"A fine welcome this is. I think a woman is hot for me and she falls asleep. Wake up, you bone-idle lazy lover," the voice out of nowhere commanded. She moaned softly as the phantom became more demanding and ever more coaxing.

This soft gauzy dream evaporated when covers disappeared from her legs. An unerring hand slid underneath her nightgown, taking possession of her thigh. Long needles of arousal shot down her limbs, curling deeply within her. Her eyes fluttered open. Amused silvered-gray eyes and a rugged, lean face filled her vision. Her eyes widened with alarm. He had arrived.

"I don't like sudden passes," she murmured.

"There's nothing sudden about this. We've been engaged in foreplay for more than two months." She smiled sleepily in spite of herself.

His silvery gaze slid over the inviting picture she made. The thin straps of her nightgown had slipped down her arms, its plunging neckline exposing the generous swell of her breasts. The pushed-up skirt revealed long legs and tempting thighs.

"I thought you weren't coming."

"I'm here."

"Enjoying the view?" she taunted softly.

A wry smile curved his sensual mouth. "I've been enjoying the view since the first time I clapped eyes on you." He rose from the side of the bed and stood towering over her, unbuttoning and shrugging out of his shirt. A few flicks of his hand and his pants were off.

She propped herself up on an elbow to survey him sleepily. "I was lying here waiting for you for hours. Why are you so late?"

"I've been out chasing two suspects since early this morning. We finally caught up with them in Coconut Grove. We arrested them and took them in and questioned them. I should have told them to hurry up and confess because the woman I've been trying like hell to make love to had finally said yes and was waiting for me."

"And they didn't cooperate, hurry things along?" She lifted an eyebrow. Her long chestnut hair tumbled around her face.

His gaze drifted over her. With one lithe motion he leaned over, caught hold of both her arms, lifted her and dragged her out of bed, until she was standing in front of him.

"Nicole," he breathed into her hair. "I want you so much," he murmured against her mouth. "I love you. Always remember that no matter what happens."

She lifted her arms, sliding them around his neck. "I could never forget it if I tried." Strong emotions choked off further response. Her outward show of supreme confidence didn't match the doubts that still lay deep in her heart. She didn't know where this burning love was taking them. All she knew was that she couldn't fight it anymore. She didn't have the strength or the will. His mouth opened on her lips, taking them with a bold sensuality. The space between them became highly charged. This raw need between them consumed her. They kissed like lovers separated for years, a wild fervor springing between them.

"What about protection?" His question was fired low and quick, while there was still time.

"We're all right," she breathed against the corner of his mouth, not fighting the waves of sensation rolling over her.

He held her away, his hands shaking. "Let's take this off. I want to look at you."

The slender straps of the nightgown began a long slow journey off her shoulders. He lowered his head and kissed her bared shoulders. The satin garment slithered to the floor. She stepped out of it. With an abstracted look of desire on his face, she watched him slowly devouring each inch. It was the look in his eyes that aroused her even more. To be desired with such intensity was the strongest aphrodisiac, the most exciting thing.

"No regrets in the morning," he breathed while his hands moved compulsively on the curve of her hips.

"None." For a more complete answer she turned in to the ardent hunger of his kiss. His arms tightened around her. His hands moved down the curve of her spine, nudging her into the thrust of his thighs. A trembling weakness attacked her knees. The exquisite torment began, mounting between them. With one hand cupping the soft rounded cheeks of her bottom he made a rough sound of passion deep in his throat, then backed her toward the bed.

A medal on a chain swung hypnotically in front of her eyes as Jake pressed her down on the bed. His mouth teased the sensitive taut nipples of her breasts, spurring on desire. When he lifted his head, his eyes were narrowed slits. She locked her arms tightly around the corded muscles of his neck, pulling his head down. Long pent-up passion broke loose. Their kisses became rougher and rougher. His hands locked her into position beneath him—there was no need for lengthy foreplay; they were both primed and ready. The thrust of male urgency filled her, exciting her with a pleasure close to pain as his rough choked words echoed in her ears. They fell into the black chasm of sensation. Neither one of them attempted to contain the raw sounds of pleasure as they scaled the heights. When the climaxing storm shuddered through them his mouth claimed hers in one last deep kiss. His powerful body pulsed warm and shaking into hers. Afterward, Jake's heavy body sprawled across hers; his ragged breathing filled her ears.

They fell back to earth like travelers who had flown too close to the sun. Overwhelmed by a bonding, a physical union so intense, Nicole breathed his name in soft disbelieving tones, then lay drifting on the more peaceful plane of sated passion, stunned by the depths and heights of their need for each other that reached beyond the physical. A new golden world had been revealed that she had never traveled in before. Already she was wondering when they could travel there again. What was more, she had never experienced anything like this deep hunger for a man before. Was it the same for him? To know his possession was heaven. She'd become enslaved by her infatuation with everything about him—the way he talked, the way he moved, the way his body felt when she was under him. She felt a burning love for him that transcended everything else and threw all caution to the winds.

They slept wrapped in each other's body heat. As they drifted in slumber side by side, her head rested near the curve of his neck. His body closely molded her into him, his long leg hooked over hers and his hand claimed her hip. During the night he reached for her again. When his body covered hers again, they kissed passionately as if they couldn't get enough of each other. He entered her almost roughly, sliding his hands beneath her hips to accommodate him. Pleasure seared through them. The excitement slowly built. Everything fell away except the black void of mounting pleasure escalating inside them. The grinding thrust of him, the quickening deep inside her, tormented them both with the familiar spiraling pleasure. His mouth dominated hers, echoing the thrust of his body. Her hands clenched. His face contorted with pleasure. They groaned at the exquisite surfeit, both of them drowning in quivering waves as they reached the peaks once again. Deep sleep engulfed them.

When Nicole awoke, she felt confused for a disoriented moment. Then, memories of the iridescent night came flooding back. She felt different. The sight of the man lying beside her, who had made all the difference, warmed her. She moaned and rolled over on her side burying her face into the pillow. The brawny body of sinew and muscle sprawled next to her filled her with a sense of peace, but she couldn't drift back to sleep.

Who had done the capturing? Had he captured her or had she captured him? It was hard to tell. But it was an irrefutable fact that she had allowed this man into her life. Her mind began examining the night before. She turned over to gaze at him. He was sleeping with one arm thrown across his eyes. Raising herself on one elbow, she moved closer to get a better look, clutching the sheet to her bared breasts. Suddenly a powerful arm shot up, seizing her by the back of her hair. Looking up at her through sleep-slitted eyes, he dragged her down to his level.

"Something on your mind?" his morning voice rasped. Laughter lurked behind those eyes.

"I was just wondering about us."

"Looking for a repeat performance?"

She shook her head.

"Liar," he said softly. "What's there to wonder about?"

"Just wondering how we're eventually going to wind up."

For the briefest moment, his eyes clouded, then they cleared. His hand tugged on her hair gently. "Remember one thing, and all the rest will take care of itself."

"What's that?"

"I love you."

She knew with every feminine instinct deep inside her that he meant what he said. She smiled at him. "Hungry for breakfast?" she queried.

He didn't answer her question. Instead he continued drinking her in with his eyes. "You look good in the morning. Young and vulnerable and very accessible. Did you know that?" he teased, nudging her legs apart. Laughter rumbled up from deep inside him. Rolling over, he pinned her beneath him. Once again she was reminded of his superior strength.

Gazing up at him, she protested softly. "We need to get up. There's a repairman coming today to look at the air conditioner. It's not running properly. What have you got to do today?'' It was Saturday morning and she wasn't sure whether he had to work or not.

''I don't have to go in,'' he announced. Sitting up, he searched the pockets of his discarded pants for a cigarette.

She slipped out of bed to walk into the bathroom. Studying herself in the mirror, she saw that her face looked ravaged by sleep and lovemaking, but her green eyes shone with pleasure, like those of a cat that had gotten to the cream of life. Disheveled but glowing with the look of a woman who had been thoroughly made love to, she ran the water to the shower.

When she emerged, she wrapped herself in her terry robe and tied the belt around her waist, then she ran a brush through her hair. When she came out, Jake had slipped on his pants but that was all. His naked torso was hunched over, with his forearms resting on spread knees. His eyes followed her across the room like those of a cat stalking its prey. He rose from the side of the bed and covered the distance between them. She lifted her gaze to study him. His voice dropped to husky intimacy.

''You admitted last night you wanted me. You haven't changed your mind this morning. Why are you dodging me?''

''I wanted to get dressed, that was all. I wasn't dodging you. Want some breakfast?''

''There's no need to rush around getting dressed.'' He pulled her into his arms. The look in his eyes spoke volumes and volumes, the steamy kind. He was a master at it. ''The repairman has seen a woman in a robe before. He's not going to drop dead in his tracks.

But maybe I will have some breakfast. Whatever you're going to have will be fine with me."

They walked into the kitchen with his hand locked around her waist. She got things out of the refrigerator while he stood watching. She began making breakfast. They basked in an afterglow of lovemaking, still united by the emotional and physical bond that had been forged between them.

"What are you going to do today?" she asked, turning to him.

"I think I'm going to be hanging around you, making it with you every chance I get." She shot him a look that didn't conceal the way his words affected her. A smile tugged at his mouth. "Besides it's Saturday, I'm not working, you're not working. We've got the whole day to ourselves, apart from the man coming to fix the air conditioner. Haven't we?" His eyes challenged her. She turned back to the coffeepot. He walked up behind her. "So what made you change your mind?" His voice was rough with both gathering passion and morning huskiness. She knew he meant changing her mind about letting him into her life even though she had reservations about him.

"I guess I thought it was a losing battle, for one thing," she murmured, angling her head to one side so that he could bestow a hot kiss on her neck.

"And?" he growled, prompting her and pushing her tangled hair away to expose the soft curve of her neck on the other side.

"And, I guess, because I've come to realize that others have managed to live with men working in law enforcement. So why not me?"

"Now we are making progress," he said. "I told you it was a losing battle right from the beginning."

She moaned softly as he thrust his aroused body rhythmically against her bottom. He bit her neck while his hands clamped down on her hips, the movement of his hard body telling her unequivocally what he wanted. Searing desire shot through her limbs, turning her legs to jelly. The cup and saucer in her hand rattled uncontrollably. Jake reached out his hand to take it from her before she dropped it. Then he turned her around.

"Everything's new between us," he whispered huskily, pushing open the gaping neckline of her robe with his hands, looking down at her breasts. "And I can't get enough, in case you haven't already realized that." His own lazy brand of sensuality oozed from him in waves, setting her blood on fire. She leaned in to him, luxuriating in the sensations washing over her and in the strength of his lean powerful body. His mouth covered hers with burning kisses. His hands made quick work of the belt on her robe. His tongue darted in her mouth and his hand slid inside the gaping robe to her breast, then moved downward to the soft flesh of her abdomen and below. He groaned huskily as his rigid frame shuddered.

"Come back to bed with me now before I make love to you here on the kitchen floor." She twisted her head to one side, trying to cope with the overwhelming tide of passion.

Suddenly the doorbell chimed and a fist knocked vigorously on the front door.

"Ignore it." Jake's command was low and thick.

"I can't. They made an exception, coming out on a Saturday morning. Besides, he's probably seen my car parked out in front, and yours. He'll know someone's at home."

"Get rid of him if you can. Tell him to come back on Monday." He looked down at her gaping robe, and tightened the belt.

Laughter danced behind those gray eyes. He liked nothing better than rattling her, she thought.

Running her hands through her hair, she tried to compose herself. "You think this is all very funny, don't you, making love to me, grabbing me when the urge moves you?" She sounded breathless even to her own ears at the look in his eyes.

"There's nothing funny about the way I feel about you, Nicole," he said quietly.

In the background, the bell chimed insistently. The deepening look in his eyes gave weight to his words, so casually spoken. She walked calmly past him. He leaned back indolently against the doorjamb and searched in his pockets for a cigarette. She walked to the door. Taking a deep breath, trying to put a pleasant expression on her face, she opened the door prepared to see the repairman. But it was her father's hulking, burly frame that filled the doorway.

Her heart froze. If Jake hadn't gotten her so distracted she might have realized that the repairman wasn't supposed to arrive this early. But now it was too late. She had to think quickly. Her eyes widened.

"Dad, what a nice surprise." The knowledge groaned inside her. Of all the times he could have chosen to come by, he would have to pick this one. Her father's timing was disastrous.

His steel-blue eyes locked with hers as if he could see inside her head. ''Whose car is that parked in the drive?'' His voice boomed down the entrance hallway.

''Dad, I'm a grown woman,'' she reminded him, trying to block his vision and positioning herself between him and Jake. But her words had no effect.

Ignoring her as if she were some kind of pesky fly, he shoved past her, charging into the hallway like an enraged bull to spot his quarry. When she turned around, Jake and her father were eyeing each other with open malice. She closed the door slowly, the click of the lock the only sound in the charged room.

''You bastard! You goddamned twisted bastard!'' her father exploded with angry abuse.

''Something bothering you, Mike?'' The words rolled off Jake's tongue with insolent ease. Nicole watched, transfixed. Jake moved away from the doorjamb, poised for action.

''I think you're the one who's twisted, Mike. I haven't done anything wrong, but you did, Mike, sixteen years ago. That's what's eating away at you like acid. It wasn't me who was caught in bed with another man's wife. Was it?''

Jake's words acted like an electric prod. Her father, goaded beyond endurance, lunged at him down the short expanse of hallway left between them. Jake's indolence vanished. With amazing speed and that animal grace that characterized everything he did, he shifted out of the doorway.

Her heart clenched inside her; she had to do something—and quick. Breathlessly she appealed for some kind of reason.

"For God's sake, stop! I demand to know what's going on! Would someone please tell me what's going on between you? I'll go crazy if someone doesn't tell me soon."

Nicole ran up to her father, clutching at his arm. He whirled around and confronted her. His steel-blue eyes glittered with outrage. "You know what he's doing? I'll tell you what he's doing. He's using you to get at me! I don't know what he's told you, but that's what it boils down to."

"What on earth do you mean?" she whispered in shocked tones.

"From all appearances he's just maneuvered his way into your bed. You know why, don't you?"

"He happens to be in love with me."

"He doesn't love you. He's incapable of the emotion. It's revenge that's been driving him for years. He just wants to get even. And he doesn't care how the hell he does it. Tell her, Jake."

Nicole looked to Jake in total confusion, waiting for him to vehemently deny everything. Jake stared back in stony silence. The white tautness of his expression revealed to her that something was terribly wrong. She couldn't figure out what.

"One of us is crazy. Only it's not me." Nicole laughed softly on a rising bubble of hysteria. "What's going on here? I have a right to know."

Her father's face was contorted with contempt. He turned his head sideways, his eyes glittering with rage. "You're the one who's crazy, Nicole. Choosing this cool calculating bastard. He's been walking around for sixteen years with a grudge. He doesn't have any feelings for you, Nicole. Don't kid yourself for a minute that he has. If he's told you that he does, he's lying through his teeth.''

Nicole stared silently at her father, then turned her head to Jake with questions in her eyes. Panic began to eddy deep within her. Why didn't he deny what her father was saying? What was holding him back? She turned back to her father.

''Why would he want to use me to get at you?'' Her voice wavered as she put the question to her father.

For a moment her father looked crestfallen. He dragged in a ragged breath. Even after all these years he found it infinitely difficult to say what he knew he had to say. It had to be forced from him.

Jake's insinuating tones prodded him again. ''Yeah. Why don't you tell her, Mike? Tell her about the affair you had with my mother. Don't forget to tell her what happened when it was over.''

By now the whole atmosphere had a surreal feeling. Words were flying over her head. The crooning menace in Jake's voice indicated he was on the edge of losing his temper. Her father started to go for Jake, but checked himself rigidly.

''Tell her, dammit. I've been waiting to hear this for sixteen years.''

Her father took hold of her arm, turning her toward him, but her dazed attention was still on Jake, waiting for him to deny what her father had said. But he said nothing. Her heart clenched inside her again. The nameless fears within her nipped at her, like a pack of wolves bringing down a frantic victim. No, it couldn't be true.

Her father looked at her. His gaze dropped. She could see what this was costing him. He dragged in a heavy breath.

"I should have told you this, but it's something I couldn't bring myself to do. He's right. Years ago his mother and I had an affair. But it wasn't the way he describes it." With a rough, contemptuous nod of his head he looked at Jake, then he turned back to her. "There was nothing casual about it, but it was disastrous for all of us. Whether or not she took her own life, he's always blamed me. He's been carrying that around with him all these years."

"That *little* affair destroyed her. My father was never the same after that. Nothing was the same after that. Explain that to her before you tear me apart, Mike." Finally Jake shot a look at her. "You wanted to know why we hate each other's guts. Well, now you know."

Nicole stood watching, unable to absorb what either her father or Jake was saying. She was hearing the words. They were going into her head, but somehow they weren't sticking. They kept floating around in a void inside her mind as if her brain refused to attach real meaning to them. The woman in the picture with the beautiful smile flashed into her mind. Jake's mother and her father had an affair? Was it possible?

Her father's voice moved on relentlessly, reclaiming her attention again. "He's never forgiven. When I met up with him I saw it in his eyes, the minute I looked into them. Every time he looked at me I knew he was planning to get even some day." Her father shot a look of contempt at Jake. "Given half the chance, Nicole, he would like to take my life, but he's never figured out a way of doing it without going to jail for it."

"Please stop," she groaned, pressing her hands to her ears. It was as if the bottom was dropping out of her life. The beautiful heady afterglow of love from the night before was fading. Suspicion and fear threatened it, turning it into some sordid one-night stand. This simply couldn't be happening. When she turned to Jake with a pleading look in her eyes, waiting for him to deny it, his stony expression and silence chilled her. The older, more trusted loyalty to her father gathered strength in the face of Jake's reaction. Her trust in Jake had never been complete. She had always paid attention to what her father thought, even if she didn't always agree. She was paying attention now.

"Tell me one thing. Is any of this true? Is it true what he says about you wanting to get even?" Her fears mounted as he took his time to reply.

"Part of it is." The reluctant admission was dragged from tight lips. His eyes narrowed with resistance.

"Partly?" she whispered incredulously. "Which part? The part where you walked into my life and pursued me relentlessly? The part where you decided to make me fall in love with you? The part where you told me you loved me? There shouldn't be any *part.*"

Jake didn't bat an eyelash but continued to gaze steadily at her. "Why don't we talk this over when we're alone, when he's not here, and when you've had a chance to calm down."

The arrogance in that remark only added fuel to the growing conviction deep inside Nicole. Jake regarded her with a compelling look, tautly controlled, but her father countermanded what he said.

"Don't listen to him. You let him pull the wool over your eyes once. Don't let him maneuver his way into your life again."

She ran a distracted hand through her hair, remembering with a dazed fixation the way Jake had so openly pursued her. Had he really only wanted to even an old score? Had he really planned the whole thing from start to finish? When she lifted her gaze to stare at him again, all she could remember was that hardened, experienced, calculating veiled look she saw in his eyes from time to time. She had always put it down to the pressures of his job.

Her father interceded again. "Have you evened things up? Are you satisfied? What does it solve? Because your mother and I made a mistake? Does it bring her back, does it change anything? Does this satisfy some twisted sense of male honor?"

Jake suddenly exploded into action. In stunned fascination she watched him seize her father. With both hands Jake slammed him into the wall.

"Nothing makes up for that."

"Maybe you're the one who's eaten up with guilt. From what she told me, you never spoke to her after that day. You never forgave her," her father shot back with equal venom and intensity. "All right, I made a big mistake. I was a lonely man after Nicole's mother died. Your mother was a married woman. I'd give my right arm if I could put things right and bring Sandra back. Maybe your father had a few things to answer for. Maybe he shouldn't have neglected his wife. Did you ever think of that?"

She watched Jake's face go taut and white with inner rage.

"She was all right until you came along, Mike."

"She was a very lonely woman."

Nicole's temper suddenly flared. "Stop it—both of you!" She didn't want to hear another word. Resentment surged inside her. Caught in the middle, she couldn't understand why *she* was the one paying the price for something that happened sixteen years ago. Why was it her feelings that had to be sacrificed to salvage some kind of male honor? She only knew she wanted it to stop.

"You'd better go, Jake." She never wanted to see him again.

Jake shot her a sideways assessing look. Something in him relented. Clamping down on his anger with iron control, he released her father. "Don't ever intrude on my life again, Mike, in any way, in any relationship, or so help me, I won't be responsible for my actions."

Jake's warning echoed in Nicole's ears. She concluded sadly that his words of warning only proved that her father was indeed right. Everything he said was unbelievably true. Jake had been using her to get some kind of indirect revenge. He had met her by chance, but from there on in he had systematically pursued her with only one aim in mind. He had even carried it to the point of maneuvering her into this condo, she thought bitterly. It was unbelievable the lengths to which he had been willing to go.

Numbed with shock, Nicole glanced at her father.

With a flick of his head he indicated Jake behind him. "You heard what she said. Get out of here."

"I was just leaving, Mike. I never could stand to be in the same room with you for more than five minutes at a stretch."

Moving down the hallway, Jake disappeared into her bedroom to finish dressing. Her father went into the living room. Nicole followed Jake into her bedroom in taut silence, wondering if she had ever known him at all. She stood watching from the doorway with a distant, wounded look in her eyes. Who was this man so hard in every sense of the word? The stealthy cunning fox who gazed so steadily at her. The one who had made her laugh, the one who had made her want him more than any man she had ever met, the one who had so many things about him that aroused all her senses, the one who made her feel so alive. Now all she felt was dead inside. All she saw before her was some dark enigma she had never gotten to know at all.

Jake stood on the other side of the bed, coolly shrugging into his shirt. Neither of them said anything. He turned his back on her, picking up his keys and wallet and shoving them into his back pocket. Nicole stood silently leaning against the doorjamb. Jake was equally reticent, not even bothering to deny or confirm what her father had said. He buttoned his shirt and pushed it into his pants, the taut silence lengthening while he whipped his necktie underneath his shirt collar. Then he turned around. Cynical amusement spread across his face.

"Well, why don't you say it? Come on, let me have it. Tell me what a rat I am, what a big lie it all was." His eyes were glacial. Strangely enough, his cutting remarks seemed designed to hurt both of them. She couldn't figure out whom he wanted to hurt more—himself or her.

She continued to stare silently at him. For a blazing moment she wondered whom he was still so angry with. He had gotten his revenge. What more could he want? Was he out for blood? He shrugged into his jacket and slipped on his shoes. For a moment or two she couldn't see his expression. When he lifted his head his eyes gleamed with some nameless emotion. Nicole was so shattered she still couldn't say anything. Memories of the night before kept echoing painfully in her head.

"I can't believe you could be so low," she murmured.

"Maybe everything isn't as black and white as you think."

She laughed softly with open scorn at his words. "I'm sure nothing about you is what I *think*. You've already proved that. You're a master at deception. I think you even fooled yourself this time. Do you honestly expect me to believe you instead of my father?"

Jake's laconic words shot across the room like steel pins. "He took another man's wife, Nicole. Maybe you shouldn't take everything he says as the unvarnished truth. Do you really think you should give him your unquestioning trust?" He mocked her coldly with eyes that hid everything inside him. If ever there was a person who could cut through to the most vulnerable part of her sensitivities, Jake had that dubious unerring skill. Yet somehow it didn't shatter the attraction that existed between them, somehow it strangely intensified it. He had the power to move her to all kinds of emotion.

"Don't ever come near me again." She choked on the words and had difficulty forcing them out. When people said the heart ruled the head they were mistaken. It was the subconscious emotions and needs that ruled, feelings that weren't visible that made them fall in love with the most unsuitable people. She was reminded of that in a blinding flash as she looked across the rumpled unmade bed where they had lain together only hours before.

"I never dreamed I could be such a complete fool. I always thought I was reasonably intelligent. Love makes fools of us all," she whispered. "But you're not going to get a chance to make a fool of me again." Her voice shook with raw emotion. Jake showed no emotion. Dimly she realized that the more emotional she got, the stonier he looked. A muscle worked in his jaw but he was cool as ice. He stepped around the bed. His cool eyes examined her face.

"We'll wait until you're calmer. Then we'll talk about my side of the story," he announced with steely regard. His arrogant macho attitude enraged her further.

"Your *side* of it?" She laughed. "You don't have a side. You wanted revenge, you got it." His hands stilled, but he never broke his steady gaze. Aloof male reticence poured from him in waves. His eyes issued a silent message. There was plenty he could have said but he didn't.

"Give me the spare key before you leave, or maybe you'd like me to move out."

"That key belongs to me. There's no reason for you to leave." He ground out the words. As he passed by her, she moved away from the doorjamb, and he looked at her with eyes that said they weren't finished. But as far as she was concerned they were.

He moved down the short hallway with effortless strides. The unhurried animal grace struck her again. She stood in the hall, struggling to hold back the tears. She kept her eyes closed until she heard the front door slam with reverberating force, then opened them and stood staring at the closed door for a long moment, unable to move. Then she remembered her father was waiting in the other room.

Her father sat on a chair in the living room. His forearms were balanced on his spread knees, and his head was bent, studying his clasped hands. He lifted his head to look at her. She saw remorse and regret in his eyes. He looked weary. He had to have heard her and Jake. There was no way he could have missed it.

"Sit down, Nicole. I've got some explaining to do. As in every story, there's more than one side. It's high time you heard this. Jake isn't the only one who has been carrying it around all these years."

Feeling shell-shocked, she dropped into a nearby chair and leaned back. Too much had happened too fast between her and Jake. The way he had pursued her, the dizzying heights they had reached in such a short time. Last night was still all too fresh in her mind. Already her mind and body ached for him. She could still feel the phantom sensations of his mouth and his hands on her. Dimly she remembered warning herself that the burning love that had ignited between them had to cool down or burn itself out, that it couldn't possibly last. But she'd never dreamed it would end with this searing sense of betrayal. Who could ever have foreseen this? Who could ever in their wildest dreams have figured that it would end like this? Feeling stunned and beat she leaned against the high back of the chair and stared unseeingly into space.

"I should have told you this when I knew Jake was showing an interest in you, when I realized that the look of cold contempt I read so clearly in his eyes was looking for an outlet and would turn into something else. But I was too ashamed. How does a man tell his daughter something like this? As mad as I got, I couldn't bring myself to do it. In truth, Nicole, I don't think I ever forgave myself for Sandra's death."

Without looking at her he continued, while she stared into space, listening reluctantly. "The first thing I want you to know is that it was no casual affair. I met her while I was working on a case. We were questioning people in the neighborhood where she lived. I went to her house and she answered the door. It was only a few months after your mother died. Your mother and I had plenty of differences, but that didn't mean I wasn't miserable and lonely when she was gone. There was a big hole in my life. Sandra was very beautiful, but it was much more than that. There was a look in her eyes that said she was lonely, too, just as lonely as I was. We saw it in each other immediately. Because of it there was an instant strong attraction. We were both very much aware of it. I was on duty, and I never said anything or put a foot out of line. I saw the wedding ring on her finger. We both turned away from the temptation that was confronting us."

He dragged in a deep breath, then continued. "But then one day when I was off duty and I was driving down one of the main roads, I saw a woman struggling to change a tire on a car. The jack wasn't situated right. She could get seriously hurt, I remember thinking, so I stopped my car to give her a hand. She turned around. There she was. That indefinable something surged between us again. It was as if fate had deliberately thrown us together. I changed the tire for her. This time neither of us was strong enough to resist the temptation. In way of a thank-you she invited me for a cup of coffee. I started to say no, knowing I should say no, but there was that look in her eyes that made me want to accept the invitation. I kidded myself that it was just for a little human companionship and a harmless cup of coffee. We stopped at a nearby restaurant and we talked and we talked. Soon we were making a habit of meeting *just for coffee,* convincing ourselves it was all pretty innocent. Pie and coffee and conversation.

"Then the inevitable happened, I asked her out one evening. Soon after that we became lovers and eventually we were caught. The tragedy was that it was Jake who caught us."

Nicole turned her head sharply, struck with the full realization of what that confrontation must have been like for all of them.

Holding her gaze, her father continued. "Her husband was always putting together big real estate deals. He was gone for weeks at a time. Jake was in a nearby prep school at the time. One weekend he was staying with a friend, or so we thought. Something unforeseen happened. It's always the things that we don't see coming that trip us up. To make a long story shorter, Jake came back early and caught us in bed in the act of making love. I'll never forget the look on his face. You can imagine his reaction. He physically attacked me. It was all I could do to hold him off without hurting him. He was a gangling teenager, but he could pack a punch.''

Her father remembered all this with a twist to his mouth. He looked at Nicole for a moment, then went on. "I think he would have killed me if there had been a gun in the house, but I held him off until finally he broke free and tore out of the house. No one saw him for about twenty-four hours. Sandra was nearly hysterical with worry and remorse, not knowing what had happened to him. Naturally when Jake finally turned up, nothing we could do or say would change the situation. Sandra never really recovered. She blamed herself for everything, especially for the way she felt she had let down her son. To make matters worse, Jake wouldn't speak to her. He never forgave either of us. He's been carrying around a grudge against both of us inside him all these years. I think it's part of what makes him such a first-rate detective.''

Her father laughed wryly at his own observation, then he looked at Nicole pointedly. "I want you to know, Nicole, that I begged Sandra to marry me. I really loved her. But she wouldn't leave her husband or Jake. She said she had to try and make it up to them somehow. I never saw her again. No one knows for sure if she took her own life or if it was an accident. I didn't find out until months later that she had died. The housekeeper told me. Her memory still possesses a part of me. I tried to put it all behind me. Time heals all wounds. That's what people say. Maybe it does. But what they forgot to add is that nasty scars remain behind in people.''

Her father rose from the chair and looked down at her. "I always had a feeling that Jake and I would run into each other again someday. I thought maybe the years and maturity might have mellowed his attitude, that he might have reasoned things out for himself and saw that there were faults on all sides. But when I finally did meet up with him again and saw that cold contempt in his expression, I knew it was only a matter of time before he found a way of getting even. What way he would use to get even I wasn't sure, until I realized he was after you."

Her father's voice faded but Nicole still felt numb. It would take time for everything to sink in.

"I wish you had told me all this before." Nicole said. "It would have made all the difference." She looked up at her father and then wondered if it would have. Her attraction to Jake had been so swift, so sure and so intense and so complete, she wondered if she had known if even that would have made any difference.

"As I already said, I was too ashamed to tell you. I thought your feelings for Richard would keep you away from him. I kept hoping that you would see Jake for what he is."

Nicole walked to the patio doors and gazed out for a moment, then turned around to face him candidly. "I was completely taken in. I guess everybody has to make a fool of themselves at least once in their lives." She laughed softly at herself. "When it came to be my turn, I did it with flying colors." She could have added how she had enjoyed every minute, but for her father's sake she didn't. Her eyes glistened with tears. "I never dreamed I could be quite this stupid, quite this blind. He didn't have to use much force, a little ingenuity that was all. I never met a man with so much ingenuity. But confronted with the choices, I played right into his hands. I should think he's pretty proud of himself, and walking around with a little swagger.''

''Somehow I don't think so.'' She saw her father's eyes narrow speculatively. She wasn't going to disagree with him, but she didn't think Jake regretted anything.

''Don't torture yourself with self-recriminations,'' her father said wearily, rubbing the back of his neck. ''I know from experience it doesn't change anything. Do you know how many times I told myself that if only I had never responded to that look in Sandra's eyes and she had never responded to the look in mine, none of this would have happened? When I think back I could have had plenty of other women. Why did I ever take another man's wife?''

Nicole knew the answer. But who could explain the tyranny of strong emotions that made us choose one person over another, no matter how risky it was? Those emotions that we weren't always fully aware of, those unspoken needs, that we found answered in another person even if he or she was in some way off limits.

''Maybe if I had never agreed to that cup of coffee with Sandra you would still be cooking dinner for Richard, and I would still be trying to talk you into marrying him.'' He shook his head ruefully.

''I don't think I would ever have gotten around to marrying Richard, no matter how long we went out together. There was always something holding me back. Meeting Jake only opened my eyes to what it was. I know what it is now." Her voice choked on the words, because she feared she had lost it.

Her father got up. "I'd better go. I'm sorry, Nicole. There's nothing else that I can say." There was a beaten look in his eyes.

As he turned to leave, she caught his arm. "Dad," she whispered.

"What?"

"I'm still glad you're my father."

Too overcome to speak, her father couldn't respond. The door slammed behind him.

Nicole swung around. She could forgive her father. He had never meant to hurt her. But with Jake it was a different story. From what she could see he had deliberately set out to hurt her. Either that or he had no feelings. Did he have any feelings? She had asked herself that question once before.

She decided she had to get out. A change of scene was what she desperately needed. Picking up the phone, she called her old friend Jessica and asked her if she wanted to do some shopping, then see a film or something.

The quality of Nicole's voice obviously signaled low spirits. Jessica promised to pick up Nicole in twenty minutes.

Chapter 10

"So Macho Man turned out to be Sid Slime. He sounded kind of promising to me." Jessica smiled with irrepressible charm and wit. It was contagious. Nicole found herself smiling in spite of her state of mind.

"He was a master at deception," she reflected out loud. She hadn't told Jessica just how much he had deceived her. There were some things you couldn't tell even the closest friend. It was just too painful and embarrassing, and besides she wanted to forget. It was healthier that way.

They walked around the mall spending money with a vengeance. Shopping was a panacea for all women of all ages. It took your mind off things, Nicole reflected as she and Jessica plunged into the nearest specialty shop to do some really serious shopping. It restored her sense of emotional balance. Unfortunately it didn't have such a beneficial effect on the balance in her checkbook. When she saw the numbers diminishing with mind-boggling speed, she called a halt to the shopping expedition.

After a light meal they went to a film. By the end of the film her spirits had lifted, and the time spent with Jessica had given her mind a rest. She even laughed with Jessica, who made hilarious comments about her own love life and how it had run amok. Though Nicole's sense of perspective had been restored, there was still a lingering wounded look in her eyes when she returned home late that evening. She had taken a battering and she wanted it never to happen again.

The next morning at six-thirty the static of the police radio awakened Nicole, filling her in on what had transpired the night before. Her day began with a string of homicides and one report on a missing person.

She drove to the scene of the first homicide. Spending about an hour making notes, she interviewed the available witnesses still lingering around the scene of the crime. With a sense of relief she noted that Jake wasn't working on this one. She hoped she could avoid him for a while. She knew they would eventually run into each other, but she wanted a breathing space. Then the thought crossed her mind that she could ask Malcolm to take her off the police beat. The thought played in her mind off and on all day long, as she mulled it over.

After she had made the rounds she drove back to the newsroom. Then she began the endless telephone calls checking out leads, painstakingly gathering facts. In the afternoon she went to the morgue to find out what an autopsy had disclosed, then back in the newsroom she listened on the telephone to another lead on a missing person. Her job was like some giant fascinating jigsaw puzzle. She had to fit together all the pieces. But it was infinitely more interesting trying to fit together the pieces of someone's shattered life than any ordinary puzzle. Conclusions had to be drawn, endings found to these unfinished stories to satisfy the reader.

Leaning back for a moment, Nicole gazed wistfully across the newsroom. Her own life didn't look so hot at the moment. Why couldn't she put together the pieces of her own life into a more pleasing shape, and come up with a happy ending? But at the moment it didn't look like a very promising possibility.

The telephone on her desk buzzed and she picked it up. As if he had been tuned into her thoughts, Jake's voice rolled over the line.

"We need to talk. Have you cooled down yet?"

She stared at the phone silently with a lump forming in her throat. Then she slammed down the receiver. A heat rose up inside her. For a few minutes she couldn't concentrate on anything as she struggled to suppress the images her mind threw up.

That night Jake attempted to reach Nicole at home. Once again she put the phone down without speaking to him. The next day he tried again at work. There were no more calls after that.

She told herself that was the way she wanted it, a clean break. But she noticed when she got home every night she felt more exhausted than she had been the first week on the police beat. Somehow discovering the reason why Jake had pursued her so ardently had been like letting the air out of a balloon. She had come back down to earth with such a thud that during the day she dragged listlessly around. When she finally dropped into bed these nights her eyes closed as soon as she hit the pillows. Especially when she reminded herself that she had to be strong and not let him creep back into her life again. Then all she wanted was the oblivion of sleep.

But her dreams and thoughts were still full of Jake. No matter how exhausted she was she couldn't forget him. She couldn't forget those moments in his arms. Everything about him haunted her. And she couldn't stop wondering if he thought of her.

Each day it was more of the same thing. She would catch herself thinking of him at odd times when she was driving along, or taking down details at the scene of a homicide, constantly looking for him with one part of her mind. There seemed to be no situation when it was not possible for him to sneak into her thoughts. But she didn't see him, and finally inadvertently she discovered that he was working on a special task force.

By the end of the second week her world looked gray, the food she ate had no taste, the television programs she watched didn't hold her interest. None of the clothes in her closet appealed, and they no longer flattered her. Jake left several messages on the answering machine but she ignored them. When she looked into the mirror she saw the same face she had always seen, but the vibrancy was gone from her eyes. On top of everything else, she couldn't do a thing with her hair. Slamming down the hairbrush one evening,

she finally succumbed to self-pity and sobbed her
heart out. Afterward there was anger that she had
been reduced to this self-pitying state of mind because she still missed him like mad.

Not wanting to run into Jake again and make things
worse than they already were, she decided to ask Malcolm for a transfer. She had to get off the police beat.
She had to stop herself from looking for Jake, stop
herself from thinking about him. Or she would go
crazy.

The next morning Nicole walked slowly to Malcolm's office. His door was always open—literally and
figuratively. She leaned against the doorjamb.

"Can I have a word, Malcolm?"

"Of course. What is it?" He stretched expansively
and swung the swivel desk chair to face her, stacking
his hands behind his head.

Nicole glided inside and dropped into a chair opposite his desk. "I want to go back to court reporting, or even back to general reporting. Or maybe I
want to be an assistant city editor or a copy editor and
work a desk. Anything but the police beat. I want out,
Malcolm, and as quickly as possible." She knew her
voice gave away her edginess.

Malcolm gave her a shrewd discerning look.
"You've been doing a great job. But then you already
know that. I told you enough times. You were lapping it up, the excitement, the adrenaline. You're one
of the best reporters I've ever had on the police beat.
Why this sudden change of heart?" He keenly observed the closed-in, drawn look on her face. "We've
always been on good terms. You know you can be
candid with me."

She avoided his eyes and ran a slender finger along the edge of his massive walnut desk. She crossed her long legs, one over the other. "It's Jake Slater. I don't want to run into him anymore," she said pointedly.

He raised a speculative eyebrow. "For a smart girl, you sure know how to sound dumb. You mean to tell me you're going to throw away something you're good at because of some— I surmise this change of mind has something to do with an affair of the heart."

"I don't want to talk about it, Malcolm. I just want out. I don't want to keep thinking I'm going to run into him."

"I'll tell you something about Jake. He's no angel, but underneath he's okay." She shot him a warning look that said she knew differently, but he wasn't deterred. "You can't run away from these things. Why don't you talk things over calmly? They say you can solve any problem if you talk things over calmly. One of my ex-wives told me that. The trouble is I can't remember which one." There was a droll look in his eyes. Malcolm had been married three times.

"Malcolm, please, don't haul me over the coals. I'm miserable enough as it is. Surely somewhere in your cynical heart there's the capacity for human kindness. Surely at one time in your past you were in a similar situation. You must know how I'm feeling. Can't you find someone else? We agreed in the beginning that this would only be temporary, didn't we?"

"I hate to see a good reporter unhappy, because I know I won't get the best out of her." Nicole smiled at the lovable rogue Malcolm was. "Of course we're not supposed to drag our personal lives into our work life, are we? But in this case it's unavoidable if he keeps

turning up. I'll see what I can do. Don't expect over-
night miracles. Not many reporters want to work the
police beat. I'm still looking for someone from another newspaper. But the inquiries I've gotten so far
have all been from people without enough experience.''

''Are you sure there's no one else in the newsroom
who would want it?''

''Last time I tried to fill that position, you were my
only prospect. You see what I'm up against.''

''All right. I'll hope for the best.'' She rose wearily
from the chair.

He looked up at her with aeons of experience.
''There are plenty of other men around.''

''That's what I keep telling myself, but it doesn't
seem to help much.''

The next day she went to cover another homicide.
This one had occurred at the fabulous Montgomery
Winslow Hotel on Miami Beach. When she got there
the suite was crawling with police personnel. The
medical examiner arrived and a photographer was
taking pictures of the corpse on the floor. A detective
arrived. She heard another detective greeting him behind her back. Suddenly some sixth sense made her
acutely aware of the presence.

Busy making notes, she didn't look up. But an achingly familiar, deeply resonant voice flowed over her
shoulder. Every nerve ending in her body went on red
alert. Her hand stopped and she nearly dropped the
pen. She knew the man standing behind her was Jake.
He must have spotted her as soon as he walked in. She
tried to concentrate on her notes, but the words
danced in front of her eyes, making it impossible. He

moved close behind her, his low-pitched intimate tones rolled into her ear.

"I need to talk to you. You won't answer my phone calls. What do I have to do, handcuff you and drag you off somewhere to get you to listen to me? I will if I have to," he warned.

She kept silent for several beats before she answered. Dragging in her breath to steady herself, she turned around calmly and met his gaze. Even preparing herself didn't help. The glittering look in his gray eyes, the lean angular jaw and the formidable broad-shouldered strength all conspired to strip away her composure.

"Let's get our positions clear. I have nothing to say to you apart from conversation relating to this job. From now on any contact we have is purely professional." Forcing herself to look up at him coolly, she put distance in her eyes. He towered over her. He was wearing a navy suit and a blue shirt with a striped tie.

She pulled her gaze away, in order to hide the churning emotions inside her. Turning on her professional air, she was poised to put questions to him. "Were there any witnesses? Did anyone hear the shots?"

He was just as quick off the mark and characteristically relentless. "We're going to have our talk, Nicole. It's long overdue." His eyes searched hers. "It's been a long three weeks, hasn't it?"

The question dragged up everything—the aching longing, the memories of how they had been together, which played over and over in her mind. Seeing him again, his nearness, everything about it, was all worse than she had anticipated. She felt dizzy with sensation. But with a supreme effort of will, she closed her mind to her feelings, and concentrated on her job, ignoring his words.

"Any contact or conversation we have is going to be strictly professional," she repeated.

"Who are you trying to kid, Nicole? Me or yourself?" A wry smile caught at the corner of his mouth. The look in his eyes said she was asking the impossible. But he went on to answer her questions with terse replies in a cool detached manner, never taking his eyes from her face.

To avoid looking at him she concentrated on her notes, continuing to barrage him with questions, trying to pretend he was someone else. She thought of her deadline and focused on her job. For the next few minutes the deeply ingrained work habits carried her along, helping her to function. He turned his back on her and walked away, and she went to talk to a witness, but part of her mind remained acutely aware of his movements around the murder scene. Finally the room began to clear, and having gotten as much information as she could from the police and witnesses present, she moved toward the door.

He was waiting for her outside.

Nicole started to walk straight past him, ignoring him. His hand shot out and caught hold of her arm, jerking her around. "We have to talk."

She tried to shake him off. "Go away. I've got nothing to say to you," she hissed.

Jake angled his head downward, studying her profile, burning holes in her with his eyes. He looked around to check that his colleagues were out of earshot. "But I've got something to say to you, and you're damn well going to listen." He ground out the words through his teeth.

Her feelings for him were still so raw. She was like pure pulp, soft and exposed and malleable. She watched his eyes slide over her. She hated the way he could still make her feel so vulnerable, the way he could still make her want him. So she lashed out with a torrent of accusation.

"You *knew* I was falling in love with you. I never felt about anybody the way I feel about you. I can never forgive you for using that." The words nearly choked her. "You made me some kind of conquest. Well, you got what you wanted. Now I want you to leave me alone. It's hard enough as it is. Please do this one thing for me. Don't make it any harder than it already is."

Her eyes must have mirrored her misery, because Jake dropped his gaze. For a moment he was unable to look at her. A muscle jumped along his lean jaw. When he lifted his eyes slowly, they were troubled by anger and slowly dissolving patience.

"Why don't you listen to me? Why can't you believe that I meant what I said? I told you that I loved you. I never said that to a woman before. Doesn't that mean anything to you?"

"What do you want me to do? Pin a medal on you? Because you actually said 'I love you' to someone." She watched his eyes narrow on her face. They were talking at cross purposes now—glaring at each other, neither one listening to the other. "Stay away from me. Don't speak to me. Don't even come near me again. What do I have to say to get through to you?"

He reined in his fraying temper. Gray eyes explored her face. When he drew back his head there was a hint of challenge from beneath the three-quarter-lidded eyes. He hunched his brawny shoulders and his hands gripped her upper arms. "I can't and I won't. That's the way things are. It's been that way right from the beginning between you and me."

Blinded by tears, she pulled away and half ran, half walked back to her car. Sliding inside quickly, she was glad when the skies suddenly opened up and it began to pour. She switched on the engine, then the windshield wipers, trying not to give in to her feelings any more than she already had. She had a job to do. Glancing to the side, she saw him standing some distance away, ignoring the rain pelting down on him. Angrily she pushed her foot down on the accelerator and the car shot away.

She prayed that Malcolm would find a replacement for her soon. Work. She had to get her mind back on her job. As if on cue her beeper went off, and she knew she could give no more time to love gone wrong. She was an adult with a job to do, not some sick wounded schoolgirl, whining over the high school football captain or some rock star who had gotten married. The soaring heat reminded her of the brief affair with Jake. Too hot not to cool down. Why hadn't she listened? Why hadn't she followed her own advice?

Chapter 11

Jake leaned against the counter in Michelle Gordon's apartment. His three-quarter-lidded gaze dropped to the face of the woman pressing herself intimately against him. His shirt hung open as her hands explored the rock-hard leanness of his torso, skimming over the darkening lawn of hair that grew down toward the waistband of his pants. Suddenly he caught her hands, holding them away.

"Jake—what's the matter?"

He studied her upturned face, fighting boredom mingled with a benign form of impatience. It wasn't her fault he didn't feel like taking her up on what she was offering. He reminded himself there had been plenty of times before. But the invitation in her dark brown eyes no longer tempted him.

"Maybe I've been working too many hours," he offered as an explanation for his lack of interest. He placed his hands on her shoulders with the intention

of putting her away from him, but Michelle was not
the kind of woman who was easily rebuffed. She
reached up her arms to lock them around his neck. He
shot her one of his long penetrating looks that said he
was definitely not interested and that it was dangerous to persist.

Michelle bristled slightly, backed off and regarded
him coolly. "Working never stopped you before."

He turned away. It wasn't working long hours that
was behind his lack of interest. He knew that it was
love. He had never been in love before, not the way he
was now. He had discovered what love did to a man.
It made him not want anyone else. And it made him
compare. When he looked at Michelle, he was comparing everything about her with Nicole. Tall and
curvaceous but slender, Michelle was beautiful in an
openly sexy way. Before Nicole, she could easily
arouse him. But not now. Now he preferred sex appeal tempered with the kind of vulnerability that
tugged at something deep inside him. Nicole had that
quality. It brought out a tenderness and a protective
streak that he'd never known he had. When he looked
into Nicole's eyes there was depth and vulnerability
behind all the spit and fire. She wanted him, needed
him. When he looked into Michelle's all he saw was
hard-edged experience that said she could take care of
herself. He wouldn't have to worry about guarding
against his emotions with her the way he had to with
Nicole. But he didn't want that kind of relationship
anymore. Now it seemed empty.

Michelle walked across the room to pick up a cigarette, her frustration barely concealed. Her slender
fingers flicked open a lighter while she looked at him

with shrewd perception. "So what's this really all about anyway?"

He watched her lean back against the wall opposite him. The long silk robe she was wearing parted, exposing one bare leg. She said, "I hear via the grapevine that you've been chasing after Mike Bradley's daughter like a man on fire. Is she in love with you or what?"

"I can't answer that question because we've got a little communication problem." He shot Michelle a long speaking look that was dry as a desert wind. For a moment he had wanted to deny what was between him and Nicole.

He watched the fine strain of disappointment mix with the good humor of acceptance in Michelle's discerning eyes. "Sounds like you've got your work cut out for you," she remarked dryly.

He didn't answer, but he knew the silent message in his eyes confirmed what she had just said. Shrugging into his jacket, he got ready to leave.

"I have a feeling I won't be seeing you again," Michelle remarked. She made no effort to see him to the door.

Before Nicole, they had an easygoing relationship. Purely physical, but satisfying enough in its way. Now that he had experienced something that for him went much deeper, nothing less could take its place. He was becoming more and more aware of that fact with each passing day. Frustrated desire surged inside him. It had been over a month.

He reached into his pocket and pulled out a cigarette and lit it as he hit the streets. He gazed around restlessly. There was no peace these days. He was working twelve-hour days, but that didn't stop him from thinking about her. He wanted her all the time. He was always looking, wondering when he was going to see her again. He knew he could go over to the condo, but he knew she wouldn't let him in. He knew he could try phoning her, but she wouldn't talk to him. He had tried talking to her in the course of work, but she had brushed him off and walked away. What else remained that he hadn't tried?

Somehow, some way, he was going to make her see that he did care. That he cared deeply, that it had gone past the wanting to possess her physically a long time ago. He wanted her to share his life. What did you say to a woman when you'd hurt her deeply? How did you get back to where you once were? Jake realized he had never asked himself these questions before, because he had never cared enough to ask them. A voice inside his head told him he had screwed up. But he had seen all this coming a long time ago. It hadn't stopped him. There had been no way to avoid it, short of telling her, before it all blew up in her face. What good would that have done? He would never have gotten near her if he had told her. No, there had been no other way. With cool male logic he figured that if he could fit together the pieces of a difficult homicide case, he could put together the pieces of a broken relationship.

Nicole paced the condo, then paused and gazed around restlessly. She walked over to the bookshelves and picked up the first book she saw, leafed through it, then snapped it shut. Then she picked up another. After a few moments she put it down again in the same manner. Flipping idly through a magazine didn't engage her interest either. The pictures blurred in front of her eyes. Nothing held her attention. Her restlessness was driving her mad. Instead of wearing out the carpet there had to be something more constructive she could do.

Mulling it over, she remembered that she needed more information to finish a story she was working on. She had to find a detective named Larry Hopkins regarding a loose end on a missing person that had been nagging at her mind all week. She might as well use up all this restless energy on something constructive. She asked herself where she could get in touch with him. About a block away from the *Miami Guardian* building was a bar and lounge called the Gulfstream, a favorite all-night hangout for detectives and police officers. The chief of police had made it extremely popular by declaring it off-limits. If you wanted a policeman or a detective who was off duty for some kind of information, it was the place to go to, she remembered someone saying. She stood with her hand poised over her car keys, hesitating. Then decided to go.

The Gulfstream had neon lights in the window, advertising beer. Cars swamped the parking lot outside. The realization that she was going to look like an easy pickup crossed her mind. Tossing her hair away from her face, she walked through the door. How much trouble could she get into? she asked herself. They were all cops and she was a reporter here on business. She wasn't walking into some dive.

Nicole had barely stepped inside the entrance when she wondered if she hadn't made a really big mistake. Stepping inside the Gulfstream Bar and Lounge was stepping into a man's world. Half a dozen police officers and detectives lounged around the bar. A self-protective instinct made her hand go for her press card. This was strictly business, and she wanted to be able to pull out the card in case anyone got the wrong impression. Even so, she saw a couple of heads turn and she could see some slow lascivious looks sliding her way.

The men at the bar continued their conversation. Her gaze darted around the dim lounge as she searched for Larry Hopkins. Glancing over a pool table off to one side in her quest, she suddenly took a second look. She flinched and froze in her tracks. *How much trouble could she get into?* Her words jeered at her, echoing inside her head.

The entire bar was dimly lit except for the pool table, which had a light hanging over it. Jake was at the table lining up a difficult shot. She held her breath, watching him execute it the way he did everything else, with consummate ease. The brightly colored balls slammed into pockets after racing across the green baize cloth. Dressed casually, he straightened. His hand went to chalk the end of the cue, before he went on to the next shot.

She forced herself to look past Jake, now desperate to find Larry. Finally she saw him over in a corner leaning against the side of a booth talking to another detective, a young rookie named Sean McCafferty. Relief eddied inside her. She walked forward. Instantly she sensed the magnetic pull of a pair of eyes following her progress through the lounge. Jake had seen her.

Turning around at her approach, Larry recognized her. "Nicole, what brings you here?"

She leaned over to ask him about the information she was lacking. He obliged in his usual helpful casual manner. Larry Hopkins was a nice guy, she thought not for the first time. She jotted down a few notes, thanked him and started to turn away.

"Let me buy you a drink."

Uppermost in her mind was that she wanted to get out as quickly as possible. "I've got to run. I'll take a rain check. Thanks, Larry." Her heart skipped several beats before she forced herself to look away and move on. She knew that Jake had just straightened after completing another shot. There was a fine tuning between them, a sixth sense that made them acutely aware of each other.

Over her shoulder she heard Jake say goodbye to someone. She knew he was following so she moved quickly out the door. Outside, the humid air struck her face like a damp wet cloth. The door closed behind her. After a few more beats, it opened and Jake swung out. With long indolent strides he easily caught up with her midway in the parking lot. Tossing her hair away from her face like a high-strung filly at a starting gate, she ignored him, hurrying toward her car in the sultry Florida night. The sky was rumbling ominously again. The rainy season was still with them and another downpour threatened. She barely heard it. Blood was roaring in her ears. All she was aware of was the old impulse to run, to get away from him as fast as possible.

When she heard him right behind her she wheeled around. "Leave me alone. Stop following me."

"You and I are going to have our talk. You *owe* me some listening time." His hand clamped on her arm. The same hand she had watched controlling cars, boats, pool cues was now going to control her.

"I don't owe you anything. Get your hands off me," she flared.

"You're going to listen to me whether you want to or not." His eyes narrowed, sliding down the delicate contours of her pointed jaw.

"Stay away from me." Shoving his hand away, she backed off. Her eyes flashed venom at him and her voice wavered. "Haven't you done enough damage already? I don't want some macho cop messing up my life. I told you that a long time ago. But you never listen to anything I say. So why on earth should I listen to you!"

He reached out again but Nicole evaded him. She ran the rest of the way to her car. Catching her easily, he swung around and pinned her against the side of it. The rain started pelting down on them, but neither one seemed to notice.

"I never meant to mess up your life, Nicole," he said softly.

"No—only use me for a while. Well, I'm all used up." She flung the words back at him.

"All right, I admit that. In the beginning I was out for all I could get. I asked myself, why not? Why not enjoy that tempting body while I got revenge on your old man? But that didn't last long. I fell in love with you."

"So you keep saying." Her voice dripped with sarcasm. He shook her, with a kind of tender violence. "When we made love, did it feel like I was just out for revenge? Or did I act like a man who wanted you so much he couldn't stop himself? Against all the odds. That's how it was from the beginning with us. That's still how I feel. I want to go the distance with you, Nicole. Do you realize what I'm saying? Hell, nothing changes that." Thunder and lightning cracked around them.

His hands cupped her face. He leaned forward, breathing his words hard against the side of her face. "Sometimes people have feelings locked inside them that drive them. They have little or no control over them. That's what happened to me where your father was concerned. It blinded me to everything. But not my growing love for you."

"Some people have no feelings inside them at all. They're hollow inside," she said, watching his face harden with resolve.

He knew he was getting nowhere fast. She had hardened her heart and was determined to resist him. "I've been doing a lot of thinking since that morning in the condo. You don't *want* to give me a chance to explain. You don't *want* to give me another chance, period. Because you're still running scared. You're scared of all the feelings I stir up inside you. You want but you don't want. You're kicking and screaming to get away. But at the same time, honey, you keep hanging on. One of these days you have to make up your mind. You can't have it both ways. It's been that way from the first time we met."

"Don't talk to me anymore," she cried softly, holding her hands to her ears. "You muddle my mind. Leave me alone. I wish you had left me alone at the beginning, then none of this would ever have happened. I don't want you. I don't need you."

Jake's mouth curved into a wry twist. "Maybe you don't know what you want or need."

"I have nothing else to say to you." She backed away and got into the car, slamming the door. For a moment he stood staring down at her, one hand resting on the top of the car. Intense frustration still shone from the depths of his eyes. He had not finished. He looked like a man cut off in full flow. Ignoring him, she turned the key in the ignition and drove off through the rain, running again, thinking about what he had just said.

Chances. No, she didn't want to give him any more chances. She didn't want to take any more chances. Look what happened when she had. Everything had gone hopelessly wrong.

The windshield wipers worked furiously to catch up with the downpour, the humming and squeaking filling her ears. She wished they would wipe away the tears in her eyes. But nothing would wipe away those, except time. Her hand hastily rubbed them away instead.

It was only a short distance back to the condo and she reached it in a few minutes. She parked in the garage, cut the engine and sat staring through the windshield for a long moment or two. Why did Jake have to keep pushing and pushing? She sat with her head resting on her hands on the wheel.

At last she opened the door and slid slowly out. Suddenly she was trapped like a cornered animal in the long arc of headlight beams from another car. Frozen beside her vehicle, holding her hand to her eyes but unable to see, she heard a car door slam. Someone was getting out. As her eyes adjusted to the glare, Jake loomed out of the rain, striding toward her. Water droplets glistened on his hair and beaded on the lean angles and planes of his face. Metallic gray eyes pinned her.

"You're not running away from me this time, Nicole." His tone was grim and edged with a frustration that hadn't faded. "You're not going anywhere until we have this out. We're going to finish what we started back there."

"If you've got any ideas about coming inside with me, you can forget about them." Stubborn defiance rose inside her along with her fiery temper. She watched the sensual line of his mouth thin. Hypnotic and unpredictable, his eyes danced with grim dangerous sparks.

"Right. Let's go into your office. We'll do our *talking* in the car." The soft menacing tone made her heart race and then pound with a rising tide of excitement. She knew that look in his eyes. Something had closed off inside him. He had been pushed too far.

She got in the car and slid across the seat. Both of them had gotten wet. Her knit top was clinging to the soft curves of her breasts suggestively. Her gaze flicked down to assess the damage the rain had done. She released the first few tiny pearl buttons of the tank top, peeling it away from her.

Jake closed the car door behind him. She watched him warily as he got behind the wheel and angled his powerful frame toward her, resting his arm across the back of the seat.

"Say what you have to say and go. We're both wet. I don't feel like catching my death." Reaching up a slender arm to push away the damp hair from the side of her face, she shot him a simmering look. Her tone was pitched low, and a fine thread of anger ran through it. Looking dangerous and predatory, he moved closer. The hand resting on the back of the seat flexed then hooked around her neck, forcing her face close to his. Events had left them both dangerously off balance, Nicole suddenly realized.

"If I say what I want to say you won't even hear me, Nicole, you're not in a receptive mood."

"You're damned right I'm not in a receptive mood."

"Then why the hell should I waste my breath?" He fired the words at her low and quick. "There's only one way left that I know of to get through to you." The thrust of his gaze dropped to her mouth and then down to the deep cleft exposed by the partly unbuttoned tank top. Nicole's pulse rate rocketed.

His name came out as a soft protest from between her lips. But there was no time to say anything else. The volcano of anger simmering between them erupted into a fiery explosion of desire. His mouth claimed hers with brutal possession. His touch, his kiss, aroused her as always to the primitive demands of the flesh. Once he was in possession of her body, his mouth opened over hers, hard and hungry, insistent. She returned his kiss with the same insatiable fire, her arms sliding around his neck. Suddenly nothing mattered anymore, except that his lips were hot and moist on her face and throat and neck. The chemistry between them produced the predictable volatile results.

"Nicole." He breathed her name roughly against her ear. His body was sending shock waves through her. His hands moved down to the small of her back, pulling her intimately to him. The wayward caress of his hands and the nuzzling of his mouth on her neck were driving her to the edge, knotting her resistance into a tight ball of need.

"Nicole," he whispered roughly again. With his body pressed tightly against her own, she felt the cool leather upholstery sliding against her back as he lowered her against the seat of the car. Murmured words of pent-up desire spilled into her ears. When he lifted his head, his eyes were narrowed with desire, glittering with desire. Floating in some dark place, she lost all sense of time and space.

He finished unbuttoning the tank top until he had a clear path. The deep cleft of her breasts was exposed. When he kissed her breasts, she knotted her hand in his hair, not wanting him to stop. Passion consumed them both. No thought was given to anything but the overpowering quivering urgency building between them. When they were fully prone and her long legs braced against the car door, he pushed her full skirt high up her thighs. Kneeling astride her, his ragged breathing rivaling the drum of the rain outside, he shucked his pants down his hard flanks. Shoving her lacy panties out of his way, he covered her. His voice, rough and filled with passion, urged her on. Her fingernails sank into the muscled contours of his shoulders. Pure instinct took over. Everything was reduced to a primitive driving hunger between them. It blotted out all else.

There was no thought of what they did. His hands cupped her bottom, lifting her, mounting her, filling her with his quick hard driving thrusts. He breathed her name against the side of her neck. The ascent was wild and mutual. As their passion mounted, their kisses became rougher and hungrier. No attempt was made to contain their raw pleasure until the peak was reached. When he pulsed into her she sobbed his name against the corded flesh of his neck. Her body milked his. He groaned with surfeit. Then it was over. There was only the soft drum of rain outside the garage. The wildness that had gripped them was ebbing away and the pounding rain flickered back into their consciousness. Jake's mouth devoured hers, stamping his possession on her again. His breathing was still labored, as he held her locked in his arms. Nicole clung to him, fumbling in her mind for words, but none would come. Suddenly everything seemed lost. He had so easily won again.

With undermining male arrogance in his tone he stated his case. "Now we know. You see how it is with us," he breathed raggedly. "You can't turn your back on this, Nicole, no matter how hard you try."

She shivered with waning passion and regret. Shifting her legs from their awkward position, she straightened up and tried to extricate herself physically and mentally from her ignominious situation.

"Oh, why can't you leave me alone?" she moaned softly. The old wild magic had danced between them.

Looking down at her, Jake still held her partially trapped against the seat. "Because I don't want to leave you alone. It's that simple," he said quietly. "And if you wanted me to leave you alone you wouldn't respond to me the way you do."

The rain kept up a steady drumbeat outside. Moving away, Jake finally released her. She reached down for her shoes, which had come off in the frenzied need to get closer. But she wasn't thinking about what she was doing. She was only really aware of Jake shifting his weight to one side, pulling on his pants, zipping them. He sank back behind the steering wheel to light a cigarette. She felt the temporarily banked consuming need still flickering between them. If she didn't back away from this highly volatile situation, in a little while he would want her again. He lit the cigarette and clamped the lighter shut. Dragging in deeply, he stared out the windshield.

"The way we feel about each other is stronger than all these other feelings that are getting in the way. Those excuses you make," he muttered with contempt. "They're nothing but pegs to hang your fears on. You've got to come to terms with them. What happened between your father and me is over and done with. You've got to believe me when I say that I love you, Nicole. What began as a quest for revenge changed along the way. I wasn't lying to you when I told you that."

Temporarily lost in the compelling sheen of his eyes, she didn't say anything. For one insane moment she wanted to forget everything, to give in to him, to acknowledge the fact that nothing had changed—she still wanted him with all her heart. What was she doing, she wondered, letting this wild desire flare between them again? She hadn't had the strength to say no. Blinded by desire she had stumbled into the same trap all over again.

She leaned her head back against the car seat. Without uttering a word she adjusted her clothes. That he had begun to care while he was carrying out his plot didn't change anything. His ragged breathing had tapered off like the rain outside. Sensing her continued resistance, he leaned over suddenly and clamped his hand on her jaw. "When you come to your senses I'll be waiting. I won't come after you again. If you want me you know where to find me." He slammed out of the car and strode off into the weeping night.

The days passed as if in a dream with agonizing hypnotic slowness. But Nicole wouldn't give in. Her father came to dinner one night and talked about Jake. It was ironic, but he of all people had taken up

Jake's cause. He almost convinced her to go to Jake.
He had had a lot of time to think things over, Mike
said. That morning in the condo the white-hot flaring
tempers had dissipated the long-running enmity between the two men.

"Don't lose him," her father had told a shocked
Nicole. "If you really love him, don't lose him. I lost
two people that I loved deeply. It's true what they say
about never realizing how deeply you care about a
person until that person is gone. Love doesn't come
along all that often. Hang on to it when you find it."

But Nicole had not been in a receptive mood and
she'd ignored him.

Malcolm had finally found someone to take her
place on the police beat, and she spent her time covering the courts. The new reporter covering the police
was doing a good job. Something had gone out of Nicole's work; the anticipation of seeing Jake was no
longer there. Even though she told herself it didn't
matter, she missed that vital spark in her life his unexpected presence always ignited. She missed walking
into a room and seeing that broad-shouldered back,
the sun-silvered brown hair, the head bent slightly to
compensate for his height, the hands propped impatiently on his hips while he listened to more tedious
details about a case, absorbing them like a sponge. She
missed those gray eyes and the lazy smile when he
turned around and saw her. She just plain missed him.

Saturday morning Nicole emerged from the supermarket, the sound of Muzak still in her ears along with
the metal clang of shopping carts and the whir of cash
registers. As she was pushing the shopping cart across
the parking lot, Emilio Gonzalez, one of the men who
worked with Jake, recognized her.

As soon as he saw her, he shouted to her. "Hey, Nicole."

She paused to greet him. Emilio was stocky, medium height, with dark hair and a broad face. She'd heard Jake speak nothing but praise for him, so a warm smile spread across her face. "Hello, Emilio. What brings you here?"

"My wife is going inside to do some shopping," he said. "I get a day off and here I am." He grinned good-naturedly, showing that he really didn't mind at all.

She looked in the direction of the supermarket. A woman shepherding two small children was just disappearing inside. When Nicole turned back to Emilio, she saw a newspaper tucked under his arm as if he was getting ready for a long wait. He tipped his head to one side. He flicked his gaze over her with an air of idle curiosity. But she sensed something more purposeful behind it.

"You and Jake have been seeing each other. Right?"

Her senses sprang to life at the mention of Jake's name. Since her last experience with him in the rain, she could barely stand to think of him. She tried to cover up the telltale bruised look his name triggered in her eyes. But powerful emotions churned inside her. She lifted her hand to her eyes, ostensibly to shade them from the glare of the sun. In reality it was to avoid looking directly into Emilio's shrewd detective's eyes.

"We went out a few times. Why do you ask?"

He shot her a look that said he knew there was more to it than that. His next words clinched the supposition. "Jake has been injured."

Nicole's hand dropped to her side. Her gaze shifted abruptly to meet his. The blood drained from her face. "You say he's been injured?" The question in her voice echoed with a dazed note of disbelief.

"That's right," he reaffirmed, watching her closely.

"How is he? Is he all right?" Her voice wavered. A telltale sign of what lay behind it was in her eyes. Suddenly all that mattered was that Jake was okay. Her hand clutched his arm. "He's going to be all right, isn't he?"

"Hey, look. He's okay. Don't worry. I did not mean to upset you."

She tried to appear more relaxed, covering up her initial reaction. "I'm not upset. I just don't want him to be hurt. Jake's a nice guy."

A satisfied gleam appeared in Emilio's eyes. He knew he had been right about his hunch. "Come over here where we can talk and not be interrupted." They were standing in the middle of the parking lot. Cars kept coming through searching for vacant spots.

Nicole felt wooden. Emilio walked with her to her car, pushing the cart. "What happened? Tell me what happened," she said.

Emilio took the keys from her hand and opened the trunk. Together they put the groceries inside. She didn't know what else to say. Her throat felt squeezed tightly shut. She felt numb as he slammed down the trunk lid. She turned around. Finally she gave up any pretense of casual interest. In a low choked voice she questioned him again. "Where is he now?"

Emilio's tone softened. "He went to emergency. They sent him home. Some young punk had a gun. If Jake didn't have the kind of reflexes he has, he might have been badly wounded." Emilio leaned against the side of her car folding his arms in front of him. Cocking his head to one side speculatively, he watched Nicole. She kept remarkably calm while he continued.

"When we have a drink together we talk about all kinds of things. Sometimes sports, our health, our families, sometimes our women. Jake never talks much about the women he's seeing. But I've seen the way he looks at you on more than one occasion. I guess there's something going on between you, even if you say you only went out with him a few times. Do you love him?"

Emilio's question splintered through her. Not wanting to listen to him anymore, she turned away, but he checked her move, catching hold of her arm.

"I notice something else about Jake lately. Jake is still good at his job, don't get me wrong. But we all know something is bothering him. Lately he's been different. He's developing a hair-trigger temper. That's dangerous for him and for any of us who work with him." He narrowed his eyes on her face. "I think maybe it has something to do with you."

He waited for her to confirm his suspicions. Taking refuge in silence, she neither confirmed nor denied them.

Emilio went on. "He's a professional through and through, very dedicated. He's the best there is. But even the best can be affected by their personal lives. He's lost something, that edge he always had on the rest of us, the split-second reflexes. He can't afford to lose that. Neither can the guys who work for him."

Nicole dropped her gaze. She didn't want to have to see Jake again. After what happened in the garage, she knew she wasn't in control of herself when she was around him. But she couldn't bear the thought of Jake getting hurt. The idea that she might somehow be the cause of it shook her to the core. She knew that she had to go and see him.

"Will you at least talk to him?" Emilio persisted with a smile.

"I'll think about it."

"I know you're in love with him, Nicole. I would stake my life on it." He grinned at her and strode off with his newspaper. She watched him go.

The sky was black but there were lights on in the warehouse where Jake lived. Men were working. A forklift truck zipped back and forth, up and down aisles stacked high with crates. For a moment Nicole sat in the car wondering what Jake was doing. Was he in bed convalescing? Or was he out of bed prowling around? She knew only one thing. She had to see him.

She had reached the point where she couldn't stay away anymore. Emilio's words about his losing an edge haunted her continually. In the dark she looked for his car, but she didn't see it. Slamming the car door behind her, she stared up at the pitched roof of the warehouse wondering if he was even in. Maybe some old friend was nursing him back to health.

Walking pensively away from her car, she reached the wide yawning entrance to the warehouse. A lone man was working late on the forklift. He braked and paused from his work when he saw a woman standing in the entranceway. With the breeze playing in her long chestnut hair and molding the soft white dress she wore to her shapely body, Nicole cut a provocative figure.

"Lookin' for me, gorgeous? I've been lookin' for someone like you all my life." He drawled the words, tipping his hat down on his forehead and leaning out the side of the truck.

"I came to see Jake. Is he up there? I don't see his car."

"Car's in the garage. I saw him a while ago. Take the goods elevator up."

"Thanks," she responded lightly. Turning on her heel, she walked toward the elevator. She didn't hear the forklift truck start up again. Curiosity made her glance back over her shoulder. The driver sat with his forearms resting on the wheel, staring at her.

"Don't let me keep you from your work."

A wide grin spread across his face. Then he wheeled the forklift around and zoomed back down the aisle lined high with crates. She punched the button and the goods elevator rose. The ascent was a slow one, giving time for her apprehension to grow. When the elevator finally clanked to a stop, she stepped out. At the door she knocked softly. She felt on edge not knowing what she was going to do.

Jake called out asking who was there.

"It's Nicole Bradley."

Several seconds later the door swung open. Jake stood towering over her. "Aren't we getting formal. Nicole Bradley. How many Nicoles do you think I know?" The silent laughter revealed in those reckless eyes clawed at her heart, but he gave nothing else away. He stood aside. "Come on in."

She stepped in and could feel his gaze eating into her like acid. Her heart was pounding at the sight of him. She told herself to pull herself together. When the door closed behind her, her eyes slid immediately to the bandage on his shoulder and arm. His deeply bronzed torso contrasted vividly with the white bandage. The bandage was anchored around his chest and crossed over part of his shoulder. Her gaze became riveted on it.

"I didn't move out of the way fast enough," he explained. "How did you find out?"

"I ran into Emilio in the supermarket parking lot. He told me." Her voice was light and breathy, as if someone had punched her in the diaphragm.

"The bullet passed right through the flesh. It didn't shatter the bone. I'll be good as new in a couple of weeks."

Restlessly walking over to the window, Nicole stood where he couldn't see the expression in her eyes. Unsure of what to do or say next she tried to still the strong rush of emotion she felt. Seeing him again, and seeing him like this, filled her with a powerful urge to link her arms around his neck, bury her face in the curve of his good shoulder and listen to the solid reassuring beat of his heart. Whenever she was around Jake, impulsive behavior seemed to be the rule. She couldn't let it take charge again, she warned herself.

As usual, Jake was adept at reading her mind. "You can go now. I'm going to live. That's why you're here, isn't it." His narrowed gaze followed her.

She turned away from the window to look at him. He wasn't making this any easier. Why should he? His eyes beamed that silent message. She had sent him away too many times for that. He had tried to tell her he loved her, but she hadn't been listening.

"That's not the only reason why I came to see you."

"This is getting interesting. What's the other one?" He was lazily tormenting her. It ranked as one of his favorite pastimes. She watched him flick open a lighter to light a cigarette. The fascinating motion of his hands drew her gaze like a magnet. An abstracted look slipped into her eyes as she remembered the touch of those hands on her flesh. Jake's shrewd eyes assessed it.

"It's been a long time hasn't it?"

Shaking off the powerful effect of his words, she said, "Emilio says that what's between you and me has been affecting your work."

The lighter clamped shut, the sound echoing in the room. It was an angry sound.

"Sometimes Emilio talks too damned much. I wouldn't let a woman affect the way I perform on the job." The look that accompanied the sharp rebuke chilled her flesh. The quicksilver change from lazy interest to one of Jake's dismissive contemptuous looks had to be seen to be appreciated. She had watched grown men nearly fall over themselves to get out of his way when he shot one in their direction.

"I'm only going by what Emilio said. He's the one who has to work with you. He says that you're developing a hair-trigger temper. That you're mean and aggressive."

"I've always been mean and aggressive. You should know that by now." Silent laughter creased his eyes.

She dragged in her breath, gazing steadily at him, not knowing what to do next and thinking that with Jake it was an uphill battle all the way.

He moved toward her with that stealthy animal grace that was almost primitive in its force. When he stood directly in front of her he rested his hands on her shoulders. Her skin felt electrically charged underneath his touch.

Something in him relented. He decided to concede some ground, but only because it suited him. His hands moved up and down her bare arms caressingly. "All right. Maybe I have been hard to get along with lately. Maybe you have been on my mind. The question is, what are you going to do about it, Nicole? What are *you* going to do about it, Nicole?" he repeated, lowering his head. A teasing caress followed, down the curve of her neck.

She closed her eyes at the powerful onslaught of feeling his caress produced. "I can't bear to think of you getting hurt because of something I did or didn't do. I just can't stand it," she whispered, turning her head sideways, so that he couldn't see the tears of strain. His mouth lifted from the soft curve of her jawline to just below her ear. His hands clamped with increasing pressure. When she turned her head back to face him, his eyes probed hers. But there was no softening of the unrelenting planes of his features. He wanted something from her. The look in his eyes said he was determined to get it.

"And?" he prodded.

"And . . . I thought, considering how things are between us and how we both feel about each other that maybe we could pick up where we left off."

He straightened. "What are you saying, Nicole?"

"Let's be lovers. We're both miserable apart. Let's have some sort of mutually satisfying arrangement."

Dropping in pitch, his tone echoed contempt. "You want us to sleep together. Then you won't have to wrestle with the confusion in your mind or face up to the harsh realities of what I do. There are dozens of women out there I can sleep with. That's not good enough." His words, packed with quiet unbending force, made her temper flare.

''God, you want it all your way. Haven't you ever heard of the word *compromise?* Don't you know how to bend? There are other things you can do. Why not real estate? Your father's in real estate. Judging from all appearances he's very successful at it. You could be successful at it, too. You would be safe. You could lead a normal life with regular hours and weekends off.'' She watched his features harden.

''If I asked you to give up what you do best, would you do it? I don't want to do anything else. I already told you that, Nicole. You knew that when you got involved with me. I won't give it up, not even for you.''

Her gaze lingered on the bandage across his shoulder.

''This is the first time in ten years anything like this has happened to me. It's minor. I could have been out driving my car and gotten worse. Would you use that as an excuse, too? There are risks involved in everything.'' He walked over to her. ''No matter who you fall in love with there will be obstacles to overcome. There's always a price to pay. If it wasn't this, it would be something else.''

''Oh, why did I have to be attracted to you? Why you? Why does it have to be so hard?'' She walked away and heard him come up behind her. When his hands encompassed her waist, it was as if every bone in her body instantly melted. Potently familiar waves of sensation rolled over her. He pulled her back, molding her against his hard frame.

''The last thing I ever wanted was to fall in love with a cop. You're everything I learned to despise.''

''There's an opening in my life no one else can fill. Like Malcolm said, you're a natural for the job. Why don't you take it? I need you." He breathed the words against the side of her face just below her ear. "Do you believe me?"

"Yes," she breathed, expelling a sigh of momentary surrender. He nipped the soft curve of her neck while his hands moved to her breasts, covering them. She was like living putty in his arms. He kissed the side of her face and nuzzled her neck, flicking open the buttons on her dress one by one with consummate skill while she waited for his touch. His hands delved inside covering the warm swell of her breasts. Her breathing, like his, became erratic as desire mounted between them. He groaned deep in his throat and his powerful lean frame shuddered.

"I don't think I will ever get enough of you," he announced in a voice that was rough with passion. He trailed heated kisses down her neck and face while his hands pushed the dress down off her shoulders. She felt herself melting into his male needs and trembling with her own desire at the same time. When he turned her around to face him, she locked her arms around his neck. Her lips parted under the driving force of his kiss. The unbearable excitement claimed them, priming them for what they both knew was to come. Neither of them wanted to hold back. He opened her bra. His labored breathing filled her ear as his hands cupped her breasts.

"Your shoulder," she whispered huskily, while she tenderly caressed the outline of the bandage. "Won't it..."

"Right now my shoulder is the farthest thing from my mind." He laughed softly but his voice was ragged. His hands bunched her skirt up her thighs, until he cupped the soft cheeks of her bottom, pressing her against his hardening body. She felt her knees going soft, then the aching surge and the deep primitive tug that signaled intense arousal. His rhythmic kisses tore at her composure, stealing it away.

"This won't solve anything," she murmured huskily.

"Let's talk about it in the morning," he groaned. She reached up to clutch his arms to ward them off, knowing that nothing had been resolved between them, but it was too late; her last shreds of resistance had frayed away, leaving her vulnerable. His hard body was taut with need, his kisses growing ever more demanding and insistent. The driving force of his kiss made her gasp softly with pleasure. Sounds of mute passion punctuated the air. With his good arm he pulled her toward the stairs.

In the morning Nicole walked around the kitchen dressed only in Jake's robe. She was making breakfast. When she had awakened with his arm thrust across her possessively, she had lain there thinking for a while. After last night, she wondered if he would be more malleable. If they talked things over again, maybe he would bend. Waiting for the right moment, Nicole decided this had to be the right moment. He had said they would talk about it in the morning.

Jake prowled into the kitchen, needing a shave, looking lean and mean and tough, all those things she had told herself she didn't like. Deep in her heart she found them irresistible. Last night had proved it all over again. The afterglow of physical intimacy surrounded them, intensifying all the emotions that went with it. She had trouble looking him in the eye. He knew that and came up behind her. Pushing aside her hair and the collar of the robe, he bent his head and kissed the soft skin of her shoulder.

"Did you sleep okay?" he teased.

"When I got the chance." She laughed softly. "I'm making eggs. Want some?" She was trying to stay on top of the situation. Their talk was uppermost in her mind.

"I want some all right. All I can get," he teased softly. Biting her neck he added, "I like 'em scrambled."

She turned and cracked some eggs into a bowl. Coffee was percolating on the side, juice sat in a jug nearby. Muffins were browning in the toaster oven. She started cautiously. "I've been thinking about what you said last night. I was thinking maybe we could make a deal."

"What kind of a deal?" Suspicion glittered in his eyes as he gazed down at her, perusing her face at his leisure.

"We'll go on seeing each other. It can be like it was last night all the time." That was her ace and she was playing it for all it was worth.

He reached over and took the fork out of her hand and put it down on the counter. "Did you hear anything I said last night?"

"Well that was before... I thought you might be more amenable after we... patched things up. More *flexible*." She searched for the right word, while her eyes scanned the crests of his cheekbones, skittering away from his formidable eyes. In the morning he looked even more aggressively male, sure of himself and sure of what he wanted. Silent amusement greeted her. Along with his I've-got-your-number look.

"What you're saying is that since you spent the night in my bed, you think you're going to lead me around with a ring in my nose, like some prize stud. You've faced up to the fact that you're in love with me, that you can't stay away from me, but you don't want to stick your neck out any farther than that." He pointed to his shoulder. "You don't like this, do you?"

"Of course I don't like it." Her voice was tremulous. "I don't want to be married to a man who gets himself shot up periodically."

"Who's asking?" he challenged with narrowed eyes.

"Last night you said that you needed me in your life. You implied that we would belong to each other all the way. I thought you meant..."

"Maybe I changed my mind after last night. Maybe I don't want you now that I've had you. You think you've got me hooked on that beautiful face and what's underneath that robe."

Nicole stared at him. Since she was rejecting what he offered, he was flinging that rejection back in her face. With a few terse words Jake could wound with razor-blade ease. Turning away she tried to recover. His presence loomed over her again. His whole attitude softened. Hands clasped her shoulders, dragging her close. "No deals, Nicole," he whispered huskily.

"I just thought maybe we could have some kind of arrangement that would be beneficial to us both. What's wrong with that? Lots of men would jump at the chance."

"Not this man. Not with this woman. I've had all that. I don't want that anymore, I told you a long time ago I want much more than that." He turned her around and his eyes bored into her. "On this we have to be in agreement."

"We would be if you would bend a little. You're so rigid and arrogant. Why don't you bend?"

"Why don't you? Other people have accepted this kind of life and made it work. There are men I work with in the department who have been married to their high school sweethearts for twenty years or more. How do you explain that, Nicole?" His words made her pause, but she started to pull away. They were talking at cross purposes again, neither of them really ready to listen to the other.

"Then cook your own eggs!" she flared. She stalked out of the kitchen and up the stairs. Reaching the upper level, she flung off his robe and walked into the dressing room.

A few minutes later he hung in the doorway. "What are you afraid of?" he called out. "Besides my getting shot up."

"Nothing, I'm not afraid of nothing." She pulled her hair away from her face, studying the effect as if what he was saying was of no consequence.

In the mirror he shot her a look of wry cynicism. "When I hear a double negative coming from the mouth of a hotshot reporter I know she's really rattled about something."

Ignoring him, she walked into the shower and turned on the taps full blast, furious with herself and with him. Furious with herself because she still wanted him with all her heart, and furious with him because he wouldn't bend, he wouldn't give a miserable inch. She showered, seething inside. When she emerged he was still hanging in the doorway, watching her with irritating male supremacy and a deceptively relaxed

expression that didn't match the steel glint in his eyes.
A sizzling silence prevailed. Jake ended it.

"You came here yesterday of your own free will because you heard from Emilio that I was injured. You
were in my bed all night. That tells me you care deeply
enough. You would never have come otherwise." Nicole took refuge in silence so he continued. "Who-
ever you choose there's always a price to pay."

"Your price is too high and I'm not paying it."

"We'll see about that."

Clad in lacy bikinis she finished fastening her bra
and scooped up her dress. Walking past him into the
bedroom, she pulled it over her head and started but-
toning it down the front, avoiding looking at the
rumpled sheets on the bed, a potent reminder of what
had happened last night. Instead she concentrated on
fastening the wide matching belt around her waist.
Then, sinking to her knees, she hunted around for her
shoes and found them under the bed. All the time Jake
stood watching her with that unnerving ease that was
designed to rattle her. When she was around Jake she
wavered between love and hate like a barometer
trapped between two conflicting fronts. Moving past
him again, as if he weren't there, she went back into
the dressing room to apply makeup and brush her hair.
His silent observation was beginning to get to her.

Her eyes flashed with feminine pique. Finished, she
rose and walked by him. Tossing her long hair away
from her face in a kind of last-ditch effort at bravado,
she walked over to the vanity unit and picked up her
handbag. She shoved her makeup into it in one fell
swoop, then snapped it shut.

Lifting her gaze, she addressed him with a blasé air.
"Take a good look. Because when I leave here today,

I'm not coming back. But you can call me if you change your mind.''

''Unless you agree to my terms, I'm not calling you.''

''Well, I guess this is goodbye until one of us gives in. And it won't be me.'' She smiled sweetly, then pushed away from him and walked toward the door of his apartment, shoving outsize sunglasses onto her nose, glad of the anonymity they offered.

The warehouse was alive with sound as forklift trucks roared around and men shouted back and forth. She and Jake stood waiting for the elevator to rise. Two of the men below spotted them. Nicole instantly recognized one of them as the man she had seen the night before. Hoots, catcalls and shrill whistling accompanied by thumbs-up signs aimed at Jake soon followed. She groaned inside at the knowledge that she had to walk past those men. She leaned back against the wire cage of the elevator, folding her arms in disgust. ''It's really dumb living over a warehouse,'' she remarked slowly.

''What's the matter, hotshot? You're not embarrassed or anything. Not a big tough reporter like you.'' Jake's eyes gleamed with devilry. After turning the knife a little, he leaned over and shouted to the men below. ''Hey, knock it off, down there. You're embarrassing my *friend.*''

When she turned her head back she shot him a withering look. ''If we were *legit* that wouldn't happen.'' She stepped into the goods elevator and looked the other way. Jake slid the mesh door shut with a resounding bang. The elevator started on its slow descent.

When it cranked to a stop Nicole stepped out. Looking neither right nor left but at some distant point in space, she walked as quickly as she could out of the warehouse. Several pairs of avid eyes were following her, measuring her with male assessment. They had seen her car parked there this morning when they came to work, put two and two together and concluded rightly that the owner of their workplace had scored even if there was a bandage on his shoulder. Knowing that they all knew made her flush warmly. She got into her car with a sense of relief, fumbled with the key in the ignition, then drove off down the street.

Chapter 12

For the past few weeks Nicole had just drifted through life, living from day to day, not thinking too much about what she was going to do next. Today, she sat at work staring into space, the phone in her hand. After dialing the wrong number three times in succession she placed it in the cradle and continued staring silently into space. Who was she kidding? She couldn't go on like this any longer. She picked up her keys and her shoulder bag and walked briskly out of the building, headed for the parking lot.

She wanted him. As she drove through the heavy downtown traffic, she knew that nothing was going to ever change the way she felt about him. Want to or not she had to go and see him, she couldn't stay away any longer. Staying away from him didn't solve anything. Love meant taking a leap in the dark. It was a leap of faith into the unknown, but she had to depend on its strength to endure and carry her along. She preferred the peaks and valleys of loving to this flat terrain of nothing at all. She knew in her mind what she wanted was to be with Jake, and she knew in her mind what she wanted to say.

She parked the car underneath a huge banyan tree a little way from the entrance to the warehouse. When she stepped out of the car, slamming the door behind her, her resolve started to waver. Leaning against the side of the car, she took several deep, steadying breaths.

Suppose he's changed his mind, suppose he's not interested anymore? she thought. What are you going to do if he throws your love back in your face? She walked a few paces, then turned around and came back, her fingers gripping the door handle indecisively. Suddenly a forklift truck roared to a stop in the wide entrance of the warehouse. All the lights blazed inside so that she could see and hear one of the men working in the warehouse shout across at someone.

"Hey, Jake! Your *friend* is here." A chorus of catcalls, hoots, and one male voice calling Jake's name in a high falsetto created general pandemonium in the warehouse and brought Jake to the entrance way.

It was too late, he had seen her. There was no going back now. He said something to the men she couldn't catch that had an immediate effect. The truck roared away toward the back of the warehouse. Nicole leaned against the side of her car.

Jake stood poised in the doorway, hands on hips, head angled slightly downward, studying her as if he were trying to make up his mind about something. The stance changed. He walked toward her with long ground-eating strides until only about ten or fifteen feet separated them.

"Nicole?"

She swung around and her heart began to beat almost painfully in soft thuds. His familiar broad-shouldered rugged frame was illuminated by the lights at his back in the warehouse. His face was in shadow. Fearing she had made a grave mistake, Nicole stood in the dark near the banyan tree, praying that he wouldn't turn her away. He walked toward her instead.

When only inches separated them, she spoke quietly. "I have to talk to you." Whatever defenses she had maintained disintegrated and crumbled into dust under the power of his nearness. Only a naked need remained that overruled everything. Love coursed through her so strong, so indomitable, she wondered how she could ever have doubted it at all.

"Come on up with me then."

"Isn't there another way to get into that place?" she hedged.

He reached out and slammed the partially open car door, accompanying the movement with a low clipped command. "No, there isn't. Come on up with me. We've got some things to settle."

Knowing there was no point in delaying, she didn't argue. On the way in, more catcalls, hoots, and thumbs-up signs followed them. Nicole cast a side-long look from beneath thick lashes. Fine lines of amusement fanned out from Jake's eyes and bracketed the corners of his mouth. But he looked tired, she noted. No doubt so did she. The strain was a telling one, it had taken its toll on both of them. Neither one of them said anything until they reached the second level of the warehouse. The mesh gate on the goods elevator shot back with a clanging sound.

Inside the apartment, she walked over near a window and dropped her shoulder bag onto the couch. She swung around and just blurted out what was on her mind.

"If you still want me, I'm yours. I can't live this way anymore." Turning around again, she inched toward the tall narrow window that looked out over the marina. The window was like black mirror glass. She stared at her image, not knowing what Jake would do next. In the glass she could see him moving behind her.

Angling his head to the side of her neck with both hands closing on the points of her shoulders, he murmured, "I hope to hell you've been as miserable as I've been."

A smile caught at the corners of her mouth. He turned her around to look at him, and for a moment she was lost in the glittering depths of his eyes. Mesmerized, she watched him lower his head. He grazed her lips with his, a teasing sensual caress.

"You win," she breathed the words against his lips. Her eyes scanned the face that meant more to her now than any other in the world. Strong emotion mixed with elation surged from some place deep inside her.

"What do you mean, exactly?"

"I mean I don't care if you're a cop. If you work crazy hours. What I mean is, none of that seems to matter anymore."

His gaze slid over her face. The naked want she saw in it set her heart pounding. It was the same for her. Their eyes reflected the misery of having gone against the natural grain of things. Conflicting emotions still remained inside them both. But they were no longer warring factions, a sure sign that they could be surmounted.

She bit down on her lip to hold back the strong emotions threatening to overwhelm her, and she looked out the window. She wanted him so much she had to close her eyes and pause for a moment before she continued. "You know I love you. Don't you," she murmured. Her voice was low and tremulous with the import of what she was saying and feeling. For a moment she thought it might be choked off altogether. But those were the words he needed to hear. She continued gazing at their reflection in the window, overcome by emotions again. Jake took the opportunity to draw her back against the hard length of his powerful frame, tightly encircling her waist with his arm.

"And I don't want to have some kind of convenient arrangement," she concluded.

His husky words filled her ears as he lowered his head to nuzzle her neck. "Tell me what you do want, Nicole."

"I want something that lasts and lasts."

"That makes two of us." Turning her in his arms, they sealed the truce. The rhythmic, hypnotic kisses that followed stole her breath. His arms tightened, pulling her into him.

As he lifted his head, Jake's eyes burned the message into her eyes. "You realize what you're saying, what you're going to have to put up with. And you still want me?"

Her arms encircled his neck with her answer, and all the love she had inside her came pouring out. Jake lowered his head. His lips captured hers with firm telling possession. Molded together so tightly that a piece of paper couldn't slip between them, neither one could quench the silent pent up hunger that raged between them. He broke off the kiss, moving his lips to blaze a hot trail to her ear.

"If you hadn't come to me, Nicole, I would have come to you," he murmured. His hands cradled her face between his palms. He breathed the words against her lips. "I've never loved anyone the way I love you. And I'm going to make sure you're always happy. It's been you, Nicole, since that first time I saw you in Oscar's sitting on that bar stool looking up at me, challenging me with those green eyes. And it will always be you."

*   *   *   *   *

COMING NEXT MONTH

#445 MACKENZIE'S MISSION—Linda Howard

Test pilot Joe "Breed" MacKenzie was on a dangerous mission, and he wasn't about to let sexy civilian Caroline Evans—a woman who looked too good and knew too much—get in his way.

#446 QUEEN OF HEARTS—Barbara Faith

Rebecca Bliss was used to giving orders and living dangerously—that is, until she met staid history professor Tom Thornton. Suddenly staying at home seemed the most exciting thing in the world.

#447 13 ROYAL STREET—Peggy Webb

When unscrupulous kidnappers threatened her baby nephew, Lily Cooper turned to undercover agent Zach Taylor. But the *real* trouble began the moment she discovered a burning need for Zach's passion, not his protection....

#448 THE LOVE OF DUGAN MAGEE—Linda Turner

Macho detective Dugan Magee wanted nothing to do with Sarah Jane Haywood. She was too gentle, too pretty, to fit into his world. But he needed her help to capture a rapist....

#449 EXILE'S END—Rachel Lee

From the moment burned-out, betrayed government agent Ransom Laird and lonely author Amanda Grant met, it seemed inevitable that they would fall in love—if a vengeful killer didn't get them first!

#450 MISTRESS OF MAGIC—
Heather Graham Pozzessere

Flirting with a gorgeous man while wearing a dinosaur costume wasn't Reggie Delaney's style. And the fact that the man happened to be Wes Blake, financial backer of Dierdre's Dinoland, made matters even worse....

AVAILABLE THIS MONTH:

✦INTIMATE MOMENTS®
™ Silhouette

Ever since the appearance of Linda Howard's incredibly popular MACKENZIE'S MOUNTAIN in 1989, we've received literally hundreds of letters, all asking that same question. At last the book we've all been waiting for is here.

In September, look for MACKENZIE'S MISSION (Intimate Moments #445), Joe's story as only Linda Howard could tell it.

And Joe is only the first of an exciting breed here at Silhouette Intimate Moments. Starting in September, we'll be bringing you one title every month in our new **American Heroes** program. In addition to Linda Howard, the **American Heroes** lineup will be written by such stars as Kathleen Eagle, Kathleen Korbel, Patricia Gardner Evans, Marilyn Pappano, Heather Graham Pozzessere and more. Don't miss a single one!